FOR

SUPERMODEL
— OF THE WORLD™ —

PARTY
GIRL

"First, I'd like to welcome each and every one of you to the Supermodel of the World Contest," said Eileen Ford.

I sat up straighter and shook my hair into place. I knew this was an important moment in my career, a chance to get Eileen and Jerry Ford, the heads of New York City's prestigious Ford Models, to notice me in the crowd. But it wasn't going to be easy—I was surrounded by some of the most beautiful girls in the world.

It was the first day of the week-long Supermodel of the World Contest. All the contestants were sitting in the garden of the Ocean Plaza Hotel on the tropical island of Luzia, where the contest was going to take place. The Fords stood in front of us, Jerry in a dark suit and Eileen in a beige skirt and sweater, her glasses pushed up into her short light hair.

I'd met the Fords once before, when I won the local modeling contest in my country, Brazil. This was different. This was the international contest. Now I was competing with models from all over the world. Winning the contest was a long shot, but I was _determined_ to make an impression on the Fords. It was my big chance, the first step toward becoming a Ford model in New York City.

"During the week," said Jerry, "you'll all have an opportunity to work with top photographers and fashion designers…"

I shivered. I knew this was the break I needed. I'd already modeled back in Rio de Janeiro, the city where I lived in Brazil. I'd been in ads for a local department store and a health club. I was even Miss _Saude_ Soda. But I was most popular in Brazil for hosting a teen television show called _Qual o lance?_, which means "What's Happening?" in Portuguese, the language we speak in Brazil. The show was about what's in style—you know, fashion, celebrities, and stuff. But that was all back in Rio. New York City is the big time! And Ford Models is about as big as you can get.

"…and, of course," Jerry was saying, "we have excursions and parties planned so that you can all get acquainted."

Great, I thought, I _love_ parties. Back home in Rio, I went out just about every night. It was beginning to sound like this week would be pretty fun as well as help my career.

"Finally," said Eileen, "at the end of the week, one of you will be chosen to be Supermodel of the World. But all of you should be very proud. Simply having been chosen to represent your country in this contest means that each one of you is a winner already."

I guessed Eileen was right. It was nice to know that I'd been picked to go to the Supermodel Contest. But it wouldn't feel bad to win, either!

Well, I didn't win the contest, but I _was_ one of the seven finalists. Best of all, Ford took me on as one of their models!

I was heading to New York, the modeling center of the world! I'd shop at fashionable boutiques, go to exciting parties, and entertain glamorous friends in my own chic little apartment. I had it all planned out.

That is, until the Fords told me that they had arranged for me to stay in an apartment with a chaperone and five other girls they had brought to New York to model. It wasn't what I'd had in mind, but I wasn't about to argue. After all, the important thing was that I was on my way!

FORD

SUPERMODELS OF THE WORLD™

PARTY GIRL

by B. B. Calhoun
based on a concept by Liz Nickles

RED FOX

Created by R. R. Goldsmith

A Red Fox Book

Published by Random House Children's Books
20 Vauxhall Bridge Road, London SW1V 2SA

A division of Random House UK Ltd
London Melbourne Sydney Auckland
Johannesburg and agencies throughout the world

First published in the United States by
Random House, Inc 1994

SUPERMODELS OF THE WORLD is a trademark of
Ford Models Inc.

Printed and bound in Great Britain by
Cox & Wyman Ltd, Reading, Berkshire

RANDOM HOUSE UK Limited Reg. No. 954009

ISBN 0 09 955311 2

CONTENTS

CHAPTER 1

"Cassandra, are you almost done?"

I ignored the voice on the other side of the bathroom door and concentrated on washing my face.

"Cassandra, can you hear me? Cassandra… *Cassandra!*"

I sighed. "Just a few more minutes, Naira," I called back.

I tilted my face into the steaming water. I've heard that taking incredibly hot showers is not that good for your skin, but I can't resist them.

"You've been in there for over half an hour," Naira shouted.

"Well, I'm going as fast as I can," I shouted back.

That's one thing about Naira—she's really big on sticking to her schedule. She's got a giant appointment book where she keeps track of everything she has to do, down to the minute. Then if things don't go the way she's planned them, she gets all worked up about it.

We only have two bathrooms for six roommates, so things frequently don't go the way Naira's planned. Well, our apartment actually has three bathrooms, but the third one belongs to Mrs. Hill. It's off of her bedroom, and she doesn't have to share it with anyone. I guess being the house supervisor has its privileges.

I turned off the faucets and breathed in the steamy air. Pulling a towel from the rack and wrapping it around me, I stepped out of the shower onto the tile floor. Then I wiped the fog away from the mirror with a hand towel from the rack near the sink.

Jill Murray, my booker from Ford Models, had called in the morning and asked me to come in and see her that afternoon. From the way she'd sounded on the phone, I knew it was something big. And whenever something big was going on at Ford, it was important to look your best.

I peered into the mirror. My face was still

flushed from the hot shower. It's always best to use a facial mask while your pores are still open from the shower, so I decided to try out a new mud mask from Jolie, my favorite health club and spa.

But when I opened the medicine cabinet, I realized that I had left the mud mask tube in my room. I knew I couldn't go and get it, or my pores would have closed up by the time I got back to the bathroom. Either that, or Naira would have taken over the bathroom. Then I remembered that Kerri had bought some, too.

Kerri and I try to go to Jolie at least two or three times a week. I like it for the massages, facials, and manicures, and Kerri takes millions of exercise classes and swims, too. Back at her high school in Florida, she was on the swim team and the cheerleading squad. She's totally athletic!

Sure enough, there on her shelf in the cabinet was Kerri's mask. I knew she wouldn't mind if I used some, so I opened it up and spread a thick layer of the brown goo on my face. It always amazes me that something that looks so gross can make you look so good!

There's nothing like a mask to smooth out your skin and give you a healthy glow.

The directions on the tube said to leave the mud on for ten minutes, so I decided to go back to my room and do my nails while I waited. I wrapped my white satin bathrobe around me, opened the door, and stepped into the cool hall. I was looking at my nails, so I didn't see Pia until I'd nearly bumped right into her.

Pia had on a black crocheted dress that she'd altered herself, so it fit like a glove. She has an amazing fashion sense, and knows how to make the most of her clothes. She used to have very long thick hair, but a couple of weeks ago a hairstylist at a test photo shoot cut it very short. The short cut frames her face and makes her cheekbones stand out. So now she's more chic than ever, but I don't think she's completely used to it yet.

"Ah—*scusi*, excuse me, Cassandra," Pia said, taking a step backward.

Pia's from Italy, and her English isn't too great. English isn't my native language, either, but I've had a lot more practice speaking it than Pia has. And since I've been in New

York, I've hardly had a chance to speak Portuguese at all. Of course, sometimes it slips out, especially when things get exciting.

She peered at me. "*Ma che cosa è*? What is this on your face?"

"It's a mask," I told her. "You know, for cleaning your skin."

"Ah, *sì*, I understand," she said. "That is why you were taking so long a time in the bathroom."

"Oh, yeah," I said, looking around. "Where's Naira, anyway? She can have the bathroom now. She was making such a fuss, I thought she was going to break the door down."

"Naira has gone. She had an appointment to test with a photographer and she could not wait any longer. It is important to her to be on time, you know." Pia shook her head. "She did not look very happy to me at all, Cassandra. You may want to say that you are sorry to her."

I shrugged. Like I said, Naira has this thing about her schedule.

"What about the other bathroom?" I said. "Why didn't she just go in there?"

"I am afraid that Katerina is having one of her long baths in there," said Pia, rolling her eyes.

"Oh," I said. Katerina is Pia's roommate. She's from Russia, and she's not very social, to say the least. I don't think the two of them get along that well. "Listen, you're not taking a shower now or anything, are you, Pia?"

"No, I was just going to the living room to call Ford to see if I am scheduled for anything," she answered.

"Oh, good," I said, heading down the hall toward the room I shared with Paige. "Because I have to wash this stuff off my face in ten minutes."

As I opened the door to my room, Paige's black-and-white cat, Scooter, ran out. I saw Paige quickly stuff something beneath her pillow. It was probably her diary, which she thinks I don't know about. But she has no reason to worry. I would never read it—I'm not that kind of person.

Besides, from what I know of Paige, I'm sure her diary isn't exactly the most exciting reading material. I mean, she's nice and everything, but she's kind of quiet. She's from a little town somewhere in the Midwest. I don't think she'd ever been to a big city before she came to live in New York. And she's only been in the city a few weeks.

Paige picked up a book from her night table as I walked into the room. And that's another thing about Paige. She's always reading.

"Hi," I said, sitting down on the edge of my bed. I began to look through the clutter on my night table for a nail file.

"Hi. I thought you had to go to Ford," said Paige, tucking her curly red hair behind her ear.

"I do," I said, starting to file my nails. "But I don't have to be there until two."

"It's five after one now," said Paige, looking at her watch. "You have to wash that stuff off your face, *and* put makeup on, *and* get dressed. Not to mention the time it will take you to get to Ford."

"*Ta brincando!* You're kidding!" I said. I stopped filing. "How did this happen? I had no idea it was so late!"

I knew I had to get moving if I was going to make it to Ford on time. I put down the file and reached for the bottle of red nail polish on my night table. The brush was stiff with dried polish. I must have left it open the last time I had used it.

"Paige, do you have any nail polish I can use?" I asked.

"Sure," she said, looking up from her book. She reached into her night table drawer and handed me a small bottle.

I looked at the bottle. The polish was clear, my least favorite color, if you can call "clear" a color. But it was better than nothing. In fact, it was probably better than my red polish anyway. Models are supposed to look as natural as possible: clean hair, not much makeup, neutral nail polish. That way we can be ready to work at any time. It makes sense, but I just can't resist red nail polish, or plum lipstick, or black eyeliner, or blue mascara or....

"Thanks," I said to Paige.

I opened the bottle and began polishing my nails.

"Um, Cassandra?" said Paige. "Are you sure you want to do that?"

"What do you mean?" I asked without looking up.

"Well, it's just, um, I mean how are you

going to wash that stuff off your face if your nails are wet?" she asked.

"Oh," I sighed. Why hadn't I thought of that? I closed the bottle. "How long have I been in here?"

Paige shrugged. "A couple of minutes."

"Okay," I said. I put the polish on my night table and walked over to the closet. "Do me a favor, Paige. Let me know when ten minutes are up?"

"Sure," said Paige, looking at her watch.

"Thanks," I said.

I looked into the closet and wondered what to wear. I pulled out my black mini-dress. It would look great, but it was too warm for long sleeves. New York in August is humid and *hot*. Almost as hot as Rio's summers. Actually, since Rio is south of the earth's equator, the seasons are opposite New York's. The summer months are December, January, and February. And Rio's winter months are June, July, and August, which is when New York is at its hottest.

I tossed the dress on my bed and took out my black-and-red striped stretch pants with the side zipper. They were cute, but the shoes that went best with them were back in Rio. It was amazing. Even though I'd packed three huge suitcases and a trunk to bring to New York, it always seemed like whenever I wanted to wear something, it was back home in my family's apartment.

I threw the pants on top of the bed and turned to my dresser. In the top drawer was the black sleeveless body suit I'd bought last week. But what should I wear with it?

Just then, Paige's voice broke into my thoughts. "Okay, Cassandra. It's time."

"Time?" I asked. "Time for what?"

"Ten minutes," Paige said. "You wanted me to say when ten minutes were up, right?"

"Oh, right!" I said, putting my hand to my face. The mask felt dry. I had to get to the bathroom and take it off.

A couple of minutes later I was back in my room, in front of the full-length mirror on the closet door. The mask was off and my face was moisturized. Now I was trying to decide between two outfits. One was the black body suit which went with a short, gauzy black skirt, and high-heeled black sandals. The other one was a long black dress, snug at the top, then flaring at the waist into a full skirt.

"What do you think, Paige?" I asked.

Paige lifted her head. "I think if you don't hurry up and decide you'll never make your appointment."

I groaned. Maybe the longer dress made me look too old. Or did the short skirt make me look too young? Finally I decided on the short-skirt outfit. I wiggled into the body suit, pulled on the skirt, and buckled the sandals.

I barely had five minutes to do my hair and makeup. I quickly put on a little eyeliner, a little mascara, and my plum lipstick, of course. My hair's cut in a short bob, which makes it easy to do, thank goodness. I scrunched some styling mousse through my hair and was ready to go.

"Ta-da!" I said to Paige, twirling around.

She rolled her eyes at me, but I knew she thought I was funny.

I was all ready to go. Except for one thing—my bag. Where was my big black leather bag? I couldn't possibly leave the apartment without that bag. My life was in there!

"Hey, Paige, have you seen my bag around?" I asked.

"The huge black one?" Paige looked up from her book again. I nodded eagerly. "No, not lately."

I sighed. "Why do these things always happen when I'm in a hurry?"

"When are you not in a hurry?" Paige asked. But she put down her book and got up. "I'll help you look."

"Thanks," I said, searching through the pile of clothes on my bed. "That would be great."

But the bag was nowhere to be found.

"Maybe it's in the living room," Paige suggested.

"Maybe."

We walked down the hall to the living room. Pia was just hanging up the phone and writing something on a notepad. Kerri was down on the rug, doing sit-ups, her feet hooked under the white couch. She had on a big turquoise T-shirt and black bicycle shorts. Her shoulder-length blond hair was in two braids, and she had a sweatband on.

"Hey, have either of you seen my black bag?" I asked.

"No," said Pia. "I do not think so."

Kerri stood up. "Maybe you left it in your room, Cass."

"We already looked there," said Paige.

I picked up two of the oversized white pillows from the couch.

"This is ridiculous," I said. I tossed the pillows aside and felt under the seat cushions.

Kerri laughed. "There's no way your bag is lost in the couch—it's huge. If someone had sat on it, they would have noticed it right away. It would be like sitting on a watermelon!"

"Very funny," I said. "Where could it be?"

"I am sorry I cannot help you look," said Pia, standing up. "But I have a booking this afternoon. Perhaps you can remember where you used your bag last, Cassandra."

I shook my head and rolled my eyes at her. "If I remembered that, I'd know where it is," I snapped. I sighed. "Sorry. It's just—this is going to make me late for my meeting."

Mrs. Hill's voice came from down the hall. "Whoever used this bathroom last has got some cleaning up to do," she called.

Great, I thought. Yet another thing to do. How do they expect me to get any *real* work done around here? I thought I was here to model, not be a maid!

"Fine, I'll do it later!" I called back.

Mrs. Hill appeared in the doorway. "I'm sorry, Cassandra, but I'll have to ask you to do it now. It's not fair to the other girls to leave the bathroom in that state. You know the rules."

"Rules, rules. *Que mal,* what a pain," I muttered. "Now I really *am* going to be late."

"I'll help you, Cass," volunteered Kerri.

We went down the hall to the bathroom, which, I admit, was a mess. There was a puddle on the floor, where I'd stepped out of the shower. The towels I'd used were in a pile in the corner. Even so, I wished that for once in her life Mrs. Hill would ease up on the rules and let me clean up after my meeting. Messiness just wasn't the kind of thing I normally noticed. I guess it was because back home in Rio, one of the maids would have picked up after me before I'd even thought about it.

Kerri picked up the tube of mask from the sink. "Is this mine?"

"Oh yeah," I said. I picked up a towel and wiped up the puddle on the floor. "I'd left mine in my room by accident, so I borrowed some of yours. I hope it was okay?"

"Sure, Cass," said Kerri, shrugging. She re-capped the tube and put it on her shelf in the cabinet. "No problem."

That's what I love about Kerri. She's so easygoing about stuff like that. Maybe it's be-cause she grew up with two sisters and was used to sharing everything. I only have a brother, and he's eight years older than I am. By the time I was ten, he'd already moved out, so I'm practically an only child.

It took only a couple minutes to straighten up the bathroom. Finally, we picked up the towels and dropped them into the laundry basket in the hall closet.

"Thanks a lot," I said as we headed back down the hall. "Now, if I could only find my bag."

"Does this happen to be what you're look-ing for, Cassandra?" asked Mrs. Hill. She was standing in the kitchen doorway, holding my black bag in one hand.

"Yeah! That's it!" I said happily. "Where'd you find it?"

"On the kitchen counter," she said. "Right where you left it when you came inside to get a snack yesterday afternoon. Maybe next time you'll put it where it belongs."

"Great. Thanks!" I said, taking the bag.

The apartment door banged behind me and I ran down the hall to the elevator, nearly tripping in the sandals. But I knew that if I hurried, I still might make it to Ford on time for my appointment.

CHAPTER 2

I could feel the sun warming my back as I
made my way down the street toward Ford
Models. If there's something that always
makes me feel great, it's the sun.

My family's penthouse apartment is right
across the street from one of the most famous
beaches in Brazil. It's called Ipanema, and
there's even a song about it. Everyone in Rio
goes to the beach all the time. People read,
work out, eat, play music, dance, and even
have business meetings on the beach. I really
miss it. I mean, I know there are beaches *near*
Manhattan, but in Rio, the beach is right *in*
the city.

My favorite time to go to the beach in Rio
is on New Year's Eve. Everyone in Rio goes to
watch the *macumba* ceremony. *Macumba* is

like Brazil's version of voodoo, and its follow-ers have this ceremony for the goddess of the sea every New Year's Eve. The whole beach turns into a big party, with drums playing and everybody dressed in white. At midnight there's a huge fireworks show. My parents al-ways watch the fireworks from some fancy party on one of their friends' yachts in the harbor, but the *real* fun is the party on the beach. A lot of people even stay to watch the sunrise the next morning.

I'd been so lost in thought that I was sur-prised when I found myself standing in front of the narrow, red-brick, four-story Ford Models building. It's amazing to me that New York's top modeling agency is in such a quaint little town house. It looks like someplace you'd expect a family to live. But then again, it *is* run by a family, the Ford family.

I reached to open the black double doors, but someone reached in front of me.

"After you," said a deep voice.

I turned. Standing behind me was a guy a lot taller than me, and I'm pretty tall. He had lightly tanned skin and hair that fell over his forehead in golden waves. He wore a black

T-shirt, blue jeans, and black boots. To put it simply, he was *gorgeous*. There was no doubt that he was a model in Ford's Men's Division. And if he wasn't, he would be soon since he was obviously headed into the building.

"Thanks," I said, flashing him a quick smile.

He pulled the door open, and I stepped inside ahead of him.

"Let me guess—second floor, right?" he said, giving the receptionist a wave as we went past her.

"That's right," I said as he followed me up the stairs.

"Boy, they sure do spoil you girls," he said. "Don't they?"

I turned on the landing. "And what do you mean by that?"

He grinned, showing perfect white teeth. "It's obvious. You all only have to go to the second floor, and we guys have to trudge all the way up to the third."

"Oh," I said, turning to climb again. "Tough luck, huh?"

"Well, I guess they figured that you *girls* wouldn't be able to handle it," he said.

"Or that you *guys* could use the extra exercise," I shot back.

I heard him laugh as I took the last few stairs two at a time.

"Well, this is my stop," I said. "Good luck surviving the climb to three."

I raised an eyebrow at him and turned the corner with a smile. I knew I'd won that round. I smiled to myself, I just can't resist flirting with handsome guys, especially if they flirt back.

Jill Murray, the booker who handles Ford's new models, was at her desk. She was on the phone and motioned for me to sit down. I settled into the seat by her desk and adjusted my skirt so that it fell flatteringly around my legs.

"Yes," Jill was saying into the telephone, "I think she's *absolutely* perfect. *Just* what you're looking for. She really does have a great look, doesn't she?"

One of Jill's jobs is to convince the clients that Ford's models are the right ones for them to use. I wondered who she was talking about now.

A few moments later, Jill hung up the telephone and looked at her watch. "Hello, Cassandra. You're ten minutes late, so this will have to be pretty quick. It's very important to get here on time, as I've told you before. I have a busy schedule and can't afford to wait long."

"I know," I said, "I'm really sorry I'm late. It won't happen again."

"Well, you're just lucky that I got that phone call," said Jill. Then she smiled. "So, Cassandra, how are you?"

"Fine, thanks," I answered. "What's up? Why did you want to see me?"

"Let's take a look here...." She shuffled things on her desk and pulled out the black portfolio with my name on it that held my photographs. "I've been looking over your book, and I think it's looking quite good. All of the photos from your test shoots of the last few weeks complement the photos that were taken at the Supermodel Contest. Although I do think that the pictures Will Nichols took a couple of weeks ago are the best."

"Thanks," I said, smiling.

I *love* compliments, but who doesn't? And posing for Will Nichols had been fun. There's definitely an art to modeling, but some photographers are better than others at bringing out the best in you. Will was one of the greatest.

I leaned over to look as Jill flipped through my book. The first picture was one of my favorites. It was taken at the Supermodel Contest, on the patio of the Ocean Plaza Hotel in Luzia. I was wearing a long red beaded evening gown and leaning against a column. I looked exotic and sexy, which was just the image I wanted to have. I knew that the Fords wanted me to be more versatile, but I also knew what I was best at.

"Now, Cassandra," said Jill, continuing to flip through my book, "as I said, this is really coming together and starting to look good. But I think that you need some more exposure. I know that in Brazil people knew who you were. But here in the U.S. you just don't have that recognition—yet."

"Yeah," I said, nodding, "I see what you mean." A couple of weeks ago, I'd been up for a job modeling for the designer Milo Manning's new line of perfume. It's pretty prestigious to do advertisements, and models are paid very well for them. The perfume job would have been great for my career, but I didn't get it.

"Don't worry. I'm sure you'll get something soon." Jill looked at me, her dark eyes sparkling. "In fact, we had someone who was quite impressed by your book. And he's seriously considering you for his latest ad campaign. It could be absolutely *perfect* for you right now."

"What is it?" I asked eagerly.

She leaned toward me. "Does the name Janelle mean anything to you?"

"*Puxa!* Wow!" I said excitedly. "You mean like Janelle jeans?"

"That's right," she said, smiling. "Maurice Janelle is looking for a model for a new line of jeans he's coming out with. So I sent over your book for him to look at. And he loved it."

"*Que bom!* That's great!" I said. "I love Janelle jeans."

"I should tell you that Maurice Janelle hasn't made any kind of decision yet. He's going to choose a few models to meet with, and he'll base his decision partially on that interview. He hasn't said yet that he wants to see you. All we know right now is that he loves your book, but he's looking at several other models as well," she said. "And some of them are pretty well known. But it's a brand-new line of jeans, and there's a chance he may be interested in a brand-new fresh face to go with it. In any case, it would definitely be a very good job for you."

"It would be perfect," I agreed. Janelle jeans were known throughout the world. It would be incredible exposure for me. Who could tell what modeling for them might lead to?

"I'll let you know the *moment* we hear anything," said Jill.

"Thanks so much," I said happily. "Thank you *so* much."

I stood up and floated to the stairs. I couldn't believe it. I might have a chance to model for Janelle, one of the biggest, most prestigious designer jeans labels in the world! I just *had* to get this job.

I was so lost in my own thoughts that I didn't even notice the blond guy I'd walked in with until he was right next to me on the stairs.

"Well, well," he said, "looks like we're on the same schedule."

"Yeah, I guess so," I said, still thinking about Janelle jeans.

The guy stopped and put out his hand. "Trevor. Trevor Stone." He grinned, reminding me of his perfect teeth.

"Hi," I said, smiling back. This guy acted as cute as he looked. "I'm Cassandra Contiago." I shook his hand.

"So, how long have you been with Ford?" he asked. We started down the stairs again.

"Oh, a little while," I answered. No need to tell him it was less than a month. "You?"

"Since last summer," he said. "A Ford scout on vacation spotted me lifeguarding at a lake near where I lived in Michigan. Next thing I knew I was living in New York."

"Wow," I said. Some people had all the luck. I had to work like crazy to get myself noticed by the Fords at the contest, and all this guy had to do was sit on a lifeguard stand somewhere up in Michigan. "I was in the Supermodel of the World contest," I told him. We made our way past the receptionist in the lobby.

"Oh yeah?" he asked. "How'd you do?"

I shrugged. "Well enough," I answered. "After all, I'm here, aren't I?"

"That's right," he said, grinning.

"In fact," I went on, "I just found out that I'm up for a great job right now."

"Oh, yeah?" he said, looking interested.

"Yeah," I answered. "Something *very* high-profile."

"Cool," he said. "Actually, I just heard the same thing. They're sending my book over to a big-name designer."

We stepped out into the sunlight.

"Well," said Trevor, looking at me, "maybe I'll see you around sometime. Good luck with that big job."

"You too," I said.

"Thanks," he said, shaking a lock of blond hair off his face. "Hey, keep your fingers crossed for me."

"Yeah, sure," I said.

But I knew if my fingers were crossed, it was definitely going to be for *me*. This Janelle job was important, and I was going to do everything I could to make sure it didn't get away.

CHAPTER 3

"Wow, I just keep thinking, Janelle jeans. It would be *so* amazing if you got it," said Kerri. She adjusted the towel turban on her head. "When are you finding out, Cass? This waiting is driving me crazy."

"I don't know," I said. "Hopefully soon. If the waiting's driving you crazy, just imagine what it's doing to *me*."

It was Monday, four days after my meeting at Ford. Kerri and I were in the steam room at Jolie.

"You know, what you need to do is take an aerobics class," said Kerri. "It would relax you, help take your mind off this Janelle thing."

"I don't think so," I said, laughing. "An aerobics class would relax *you*, but it's not really my style. What would relax *me* is a massage."

I love massages. My mother has a personal masseuse who visits the penthouse once a week.

"We probably don't have time for anything anyway," said Kerri, looking at her watch. "We've already been here over an hour and we told Mrs. Hill we'd only be gone a little while."

I sighed. It was a total pain having to tell Mrs. Hill where we were going and when we'd be back all the time. At home, I'd always come and gone as I pleased. In fact, my parents were so busy that half the time they didn't even notice if I was around or not.

"Besides," Kerri added, "maybe there's some news about Janelle."

"Okay," I said, "you talked me into it." I stood up and adjusted my towel around me. "Come on, let's get going."

Twenty minutes later, we were going up the elevator to the apartment. When we got out on the tenth floor, Katerina was waiting. She had on a long, loose gray-and-white flowered dress, and her light brown curls were gathered into a high ponytail tied with a pale chiffon scarf that matched her blue eyes exactly.

"*Zdrastvui*, hello," she said quietly.

"Hi," I said.

"Hi," said Kerri, shooting me a quick glance. Kerri and I can't quite figure Katerina out. She hardly talks at all. "Where are you off to?"

Katerina looked up and smiled a tiny little smile. It was a nice smile, and made Katerina look shy rather than haughty, which was how she usually looked.

"I have a booking," she said softly, stepping into the elevator.

The door slid closed. I raised my eyebrows and turned to Kerri.

"I hope she finally figured out how she's supposed to act on a job," I said.

I'd only worked with Katerina once, on a shoot for *Style* magazine. She seemed snobby about the whole thing and, as usual, had hardly spoken. In the end she'd even walked out of the shoot! I knew she'd never get any work unless she changed her attitude.

Kerri and I walked down the hall and let ourselves into the apartment. Inside, Naira was sitting at the dining table, her appointment book open in front of her and multi-colored index cards spread all around.

"Hey," said Kerri. She sat down across from Naira and picked an apple from the bowl of fruit on the table. "What are you up to?"

"I'm working on a filing card system to keep track of all my appointments," Naira said, her blue-green eyes serious in her dark face.

"But I thought that was what your big black book was for," I said.

"That book's for keeping track of *future* appointments," said Naira. "The card system is for writing down what happened at each one." She pointed to the cards. "See, pink is for bookings, yellow's for go-sees, and blue is for tests. I write the name of the photographer or the magazine editor or whatever, what the shoot was for, like an ad or a magazine, the date and time...."

"But Ford keeps track of all that information in their computer," Kerri interrupted. "Why can't you just call them if you don't remember who a photographer is from a shoot?"

"Well, I don't like to depend on other people all the time," Naira replied. "Besides, this book is more than just a record. It's like a journal, because I write down what actually happened at the shoot. You know, what the photographer was like, the clothes used, new words I learned, any problems that came up, suggestions that people had, stuff like that."

"Whatever," I said, shrugging. I understood not wanting to depend on people but I couldn't imagine being able to keep track of a system like that—or *wanting* to.

Just then, Mrs. Hill walked out of the kitchen.

"Oh, good, you're back, Cassandra," she said. "I have a message for you from Ford."

"You do?" I asked excitedly.

She searched through the pockets of her apron.

"Ah, here it is." She pulled out a slip of paper. "Let's see...it says 'Maurice Janelle wants to meet with you in person to make final decision.'"

"*Puxa!* Wow!" I said. I shivered with excitement.

"Oh, Cass, I knew it!" said Kerri, giving me a hug.

"Hey, congratulations," Naira said.

"Good news, I presume?" asked Mrs. Hill, raising her eyebrows.

"The best!" I said.

Mrs. Hill smiled. "I'm happy for you, Cassandra." She looked back at the message in her hand. "Your meeting with Mr. Janelle is on Friday at his office. You should be there at eleven A.M. sharp."

"*Friday!*" I said with a gasp. "But that's only four days away." I turned to Kerri. "What am I going to wear?"

"No problem, " said Kerri calmly. "Let's look through your closet right now. With all your clothes, you must have the perfect outfit."

An hour and a half later, I flopped on my bed, completely distraught. Kerri and I had been through everything in my closet and dresser. Now clothes were strewn everywhere, and we *still* hadn't found the right thing for me to wear to my meeting with Maurice Janelle.

"I can't believe it," said Kerri, looking around. "There has to be *something* here." She picked up a black-and-white striped dress from the floor. "What's wrong with this?"

"Too casual," I said. "I have to look like I take this meeting seriously."

"Yeah, that's true," she said. She tossed the striped dress onto the bed. "Okay, why don't you like these?" She lifted up a pair of black silk palazzo pants.

"Forget it," I said. "The wide legs are cool but they're just not right for this. Remember, Janelle makes *jeans*. I need something that shows off my figure."

"Right," said Kerri. She sighed and flopped down on Paige's bed, which didn't have clothes all over it. "I give up. None of this stuff will work."

Then it hit me. I knew what would work! I sat up, turned to Kerri, and grinned.

"What?" she asked.

"I've just thought of the perfect thing," I said.

"Really?" said Kerri.

"Yeah. It's this long, tight-fitting dress made out of stretchy dark maroon fabric. And it's got this little cutout part with crisscross laces around the waist."

"Wow, sounds perfect, Cass," said Kerri. "Let's see it."

My smile faded. "Shoot," I said. "It's not here."

"What do you mean?"

"It's back home in Rio," I said. "I didn't bring it with me."

"No problem," said Kerri. "Just have your mom send it to you."

"Send it to me?" I asked.

"Sure, you know, tell her to overnight express it," said Kerri. "Then you'll have it in a day."

"Okay," I said. I guessed I could call my mother and ask her to send the dress. After all, this was important, wasn't it?

"I'll wait for you here. Maybe I'll do some sit-ups!" said Kerri. "Go try her right now."

I left Kerri to do her sit-ups and went out to the living room. Mrs. Hill was dusting the furniture. Pia was on the phone. I knew Pia must be calling her family in Rome, because she was speaking Italian.

I looked at her, and she put her hand over the receiver.

"*Si?* Yes, Cassandra? You need to use the telephone?"

"Well, yeah," I said. "I mean, whenever

you're finished. But are you going to be long? It's kind of important."

"No, no, not long," she said. "If it is that *importante* I can finish my talking very soon."

"Thanks," I said, smiling.

A few moments later, she was off the phone.

"*Per favore*, please, have your phone call now," she said. She moved over, making room for me on the couch. "I hope it is not anything bad that has happened."

"No, nothing like that," I said. "I just have to call home about something."

I sat down, put my feet up on the coffee table, and dialed the telephone number.

After a few moments, I heard an unfamiliar voice answer on the other end.

"Contiago residence," she said in Portuguese.

It must be a new maid.

"Hi," I said. "May I talk to Mrs. Contiago, please."

"I'm sorry, but Mrs. Contiago cannot be disturbed just now," said the voice on the line.

"But this is her daughter, Cassandra, calling," I explained. I moved my feet off the coffee table as Mrs. Hill began to dust it.

"I am sorry, Miss, but your mother left me instructions not to put any calls through," said the maid. "She is having a fitting with her dressmaker right now."

I knew my mother must be preparing for a big party of some kind. She has all her formal dresses specially made.

"Can you please just tell her it's me?" I asked. "It's kind of important."

"One moment, please, Miss."

As I waited for my mother to come to the phone, I felt a little anxious. What if she was angry that I was interrupting her fitting? My mother and I have never really been close. My parents and I didn't see a whole lot of each other while I was growing up. I was mostly raised by my nanny, Flora. And now that I'm grown, my mother and I still don't really know each other.

After what seemed like forever, my mother came on the line.

"Hello? Cassandra? What's going on? María said there was some kind of emergency."

"No, Mother," I said, "not an *emergency*...."

"Oh, well. If it's not too important, Cassandra, maybe we can talk tomorrow," she said. "You see, dear, I've got the dressmaker doing some final alterations. Your father and I have a big dinner dance to go to tonight."

"Well, it *is* kind of important," I said. "I wanted to ask you to send something to me."

"Send something? What is it you need? Just let me know how much it is, and I'll wire you the money."

"No, Mother," I said. "It's something from home, something I left in my closet. A dress."

She sighed. "Are you sure we can't talk about this another time, dear? I really am in rather a hurry right now."

"No, I really can't wait," I insisted. "I need the dress right away."

"All right, then," she said with sigh, "I'll see what I can do."

"Thanks," I said. "It's a long, stretchy dark maroon dress with a cutout and laces around the waist."

"Long and maroon," she repeated. "All right, dear, I'll take a look when I have a chance."

"Oh, and Mother," I said, "will you send it express mail? I need to wear it to a very important meeting on Friday."

"Yes, yes, dear, I understand," she said. "But I'm afraid I really must go now. Why don't you call back sometime soon? So we can have a nice chat."

"Okay, Mother," I said. "Good-bye."

I hung up the phone as Kerri walked in. "So, how'd it go?" she asked me.

I shrugged. "Well, my mother said she'd send it."

"Great," said Kerri. "If she mails it out to-morrow, you should have it by Wednesday morning, which is in plenty of time. Hey, I bet she was excited that you might model for Janelle, huh?"

I shook my head. "I didn't really explain it," I said.

Mrs. Hill looked up from her dusting. "I'm sure your mother would have liked to hear the good news, Cassandra."

I shrugged. "Well, it probably wouldn't have meant that much to her," I said. "I don't think she takes my modeling career very seriously."

"You're kidding!" said Kerri. "My mom's the opposite. She carries my picture around in her wallet and shows it to practically everybody. It's totally embarrassing. If I had a Janelle jeans ad she'd be calling up everyone she knows and their grandmothers to tell them. It almost makes me glad that it's not me who got the job."

"I can't imagine my mother ever doing something like that," I said. "The only time she gets on the phone is to confirm a party date or something. And even then, she probably has the maid do it."

"Ah, *si*, my family, also, sometimes does not have much pleasure from my modeling," said Pia. "*Mia nonna*, my grandmother, she likes for me to model the dresses. But she says showing yourself in a bathing suit for pictures is not something that a respectable girl should do. She is very, how you say, *antiquata*, old-fashioned."

"I guess my mother's just more into her own life," I said. "And I think she looks at modeling as a sort of adventure for me, a chance to travel and stuff, rather than a real career."

"Well, everyone will know it's a real career once you appear in those Janelle ads," said Kerri.

"Yes, I'm sure your mother will be very

proud, Cassandra," said Mrs. Hill. She shook a can of furniture polish and sprayed some onto the dining table.

I changed the subject.

"So, what kind of shoes do you think I should wear with this dress, Kerri?" I asked.

"Beats me," said Kerri. "Ask Pia, she's Miss Fashion Sense."

"What is the shape of the dress?" asked Pia. "Is it long, or short?"

"Long," I told her. "And pretty tight, with a cutout at the waist."

"Hmmm...*penso*, I think, perhaps, a small boot with laces up the front," she suggested.

"Ooooh, that sounds perfect," said Kerri.

"Yeah, too bad I don't have any shoes like that," I said.

"So, let's go shopping and see if we can find some," said Kerri.

"Great idea," I said. Shopping is one of my passions. "Want to go now?"

"Sure," said Kerri. She looked at her watch. "The stores should be open for a little while longer. We can probably make it if we leave right now."

"Just let me get my bag," I said.

"We'll be back in two hours," I heard Kerri telling Mrs. Hill as I ran down the hall to my room. I found my bag buried under the piles of clothes on my bed.

"Let's go!" I said to Kerri when I got back to the living room.

"Excuse me just a moment, Cassandra," said Mrs. Hill, looking up from her polishing, "but haven't you forgotten something?"

I looked around. "I don't think so."

"That phone call you just made to Brazil," she said, wiping up the last of the polish. "Don't you need to enter it in the long-distance phone log?"

"Oh, yeah," I said. The log was a notebook by the phone where we were supposed to write down long-distance calls we made. "I'll do it when we get back from shopping."

Mrs. Hill shook her head. "I'm sorry, Cassandra, but I'll have to ask you to do it now while it's still fresh in your mind," she said. She picked up her rag and can of polish and headed toward the kitchen.

"But it's getting late, and some of the stores will only be open a little while longer," I called after her.

She turned to face me at the kitchen door.

"You know the rules," she said quietly. "Now please make sure you do it before you leave."

I watched as she walked into the kitchen.

"Ah, *que mal*, what a pain," I sighed. "I hate writing in that stupid log all the time."

"*Prego*, do not worry about it, Cassandra," said Pia, picking up the notebook from the phone table. "I will do it for you. Anyway, I must write in my own call to Italy as well."

"Hey, thanks, Pia," I said. "Come on, Kerri, let's get going."

CHAPTER 4

On Wednesday the dress still hadn't arrived. I didn't want to bother my mother, but this was very important to me. I stood next to the phone, trying to decide what to do before finally dialing the number.

The new maid, María, answered the phone. "Hello, Contiago residence."

"Hello, " I said, "this is Cassandra Contiago again. I'd like to speak to my mother please."

"I am sorry, Miss Cassandra, but your mother has gone out," she said.

"Do you have any idea when she'll be back?" I asked. I bit my lip. "I really need to talk to her. It's pretty important."

"I am sorry, but she did not say. She went to have her hair done for the evening. It could take many hours."

"Could you ask her to call me when she gets in, please?" I asked.

"Certainly, Miss Cassandra."

But there was no call, so later that evening I tried again. I was starting to get frustrated. Finding a dress wasn't such a big deal, why couldn't my mother just send it? After all, I hardly ever asked her for anything.

"Hello, Contiago residence." It was María. It always amazed me how neither of my parents ever picked up the phone.

"Hi, this is Cassandra again," I said. "Is my mother in?"

"No, Miss Cassandra, I am sorry," María said. "I gave her your message as soon as she came back, but she was only in for a short while before she had to go out again."

"Okay," I said with a sigh. "Do you know when she'll be back now?"

"Oh, very late, I would think, Miss Cassandra," said María. "Mr. and Mrs. Contiago have gone out to a party."

So what else is new? I thought. They always go out to parties.

Thursday came, and there was still no call and

no dress. I had one last chance. The meeting with Mr. Janelle was the next day, which meant if my mother overnight expressed the dress immediately, I would barely get it in time to wear it.

"Contiago residence." María's voice was becoming all too familiar.

"Hi, it's Cassandra again," I said. I tried not to snap at the maid—after all, it wasn't her fault that my mother was never there.

"Oh, hello, Miss Cassandra," she said. "I am very sorry, but...."

"I know, I know," I said. "My mother's not in, right?"

"Yes, that is right."

"Listen," I said, getting an idea. "Can you do me a favor? Please?"

"Certainly, Miss Cassandra," María said, "whatever you wish."

"I need you to find something in my closet," I told her. "A dress."

"Oh, no," said María. "I am not permitted to open the closets, Mrs. Contiago has said so. I could lose my job."

I sighed.

"Well, if anyone asks, tell them that *I* said it was okay," I said. "You can go into my closet, in my room. Do you know which one that is? The big bedroom on the second floor with the cream wallpaper and the gold carpet? It looks out on the ocean."

"Yes, Miss, I know that room."

"Great. There are two closets in that room. I think the dress I want is in the closet near the window. Check there first anyway," I said. "The dress is long and sort of a dark red or maroon color. It's got laces at the waist, a high neck, and no sleeves. I'll hold on and you can pick up the phone in that room to let me know if you see it, okay?"

A few minutes later, María picked up the extension.

"I am sorry, Miss," she said, "but I cannot find it."

My heart sank.

"Are you sure?" I asked. "I mean, did you really look? In *both* closets?"

"Oh, yes, Miss," said María. "It's just that there are so many clothes...."

"All right," I said sadly. "Thanks anyway, I guess."

I hung up the phone and sighed. I couldn't believe it. Here it was, the day before my meeting with Mr. Janelle, and my mother hadn't sent the dress. After I had told her how important it was! I guessed it was pretty typical of her. I knew I shouldn't be surprised, but still, why couldn't I count on my own mother?

I felt a little like crying, but that gets you nowhere. If I was going to get this job, I'd have to do it on my own.

I walked down the hall to my room and threw open my closet door. There on the floor were the little black lace-up boots I had bought with Kerri a few days before. I picked them up. No doubt about it, they were really cute. But now I didn't have the dress to wear them with.

I sighed again as I gazed at the long row of dresses, blouses, skirts, and pants hanging in my side of the closet. I just *had* to find *something* in there to wear to my meeting with Mr. Janelle. I could feel my hysteria building up again.

Just then, there was a knock at the door.

"Come in!" I called.

"*Ciao!* Hi, Cassandra, it is me," said Pia, poking her head in. She pushed the door open wider, and I could see that she was holding Scooter in her arms. "*Per favore*, please, may I bring this animal in here for a while?"

"Sure," I said.

"*Grazie*, thank you," she said. She put Scooter on Paige's bed. "I am trying to crochet a vest, and he is always tangling himself up in the yarn." Just then, she noticed the little boots in my hands. "Oh, *che belle queste scarpe!* How beautiful they are! And tell me, how do they look with your dress?"

"I don't know. The dress never came," I told her.

"Ah, *che peccato!* That's too bad," she said. She fluffed her short bangs with her fingers and frowned a little. "Now I suppose you must decide on something else. Perhaps, you would like my suggestion?"

"Sure," I said, "anything would help. If you said to wear a potato sack right now, I probably would."

"What I am thinking," said Pia, "is that you should wear something white."

"White?" I repeated.

"Yes," she said. "I am thinking that you do not wear this color often enough."

"Really?" I said. I'd never really thought of white as one of my colors.

48

"*Certamente*, of course," she said. "White will show off your dark hair very well. And your skin, it is very smooth and a little, how do you say, olive? Yes, white would be very nice."

I guessed it made sense. But what did I have that was white? I looked in the closet.

"Well," I said, pulling out a white silk sleeveless dress, "there's this."

"Oh, yes, that is very nice," said Pia enthusiastically.

"But this dress is so short. I was planning on wearing something long," I said. "I want to look elegant, but funky, too."

"Funky?" Pia repeated, wrinkling her nose. "I am sorry, Cassandra, but I do not know the meaning of this word 'funky.'"

"Funky," I said again. "You know, interesting, offbeat."

"Ah, *si*," she said. "*Originale.*"

"Right, that's it."

"Well, perhaps we can make this white dress of yours a bit more, how you say, *funky*," she said, holding out her hand for the dress.

I handed it to her. "What do you mean?"

She shrugged.

"Who knows? A cut here, a stitch there," she said. She looked down at the dress, then back up at me. She grinned and wiggled her eyebrows. "We will see what we can do."

An hour and a half later I stood in front of the mirror in Pia's room. I couldn't believe it. She had completely transformed the white dress. I almost didn't recognize it.

I admit that I'd been a little worried when Pia had first started cutting it to pieces in what looked to me like a random fashion. After all, it was a pretty nice dress, and I'd bought it in Rio, so it would be hard to re-place. But there was no doubt about it, the dress looked better than ever. It was absolutely elegant and funky, exactly what I'd been look-ing for!

Instead of coming to above my knees, the dress now reached almost to my ankles. Pia had cut three horizontal lines across the white fabric and inserted three wide stripes made out of some old sheer scarves she had. The first stripe, which was at my waist, was a beautiful red and purple flower pattern. The next stripe, which was just below my hips, was purple and white checks. And the last stripe was at my knees, and was made out of a red paisley pattern.

"So?" said Pia, standing behind me, her blue eyes sparkling. "*Ti piace?* You like?"

"It looks great!" I said happily.

Just then there was a knock at the door, and Kerri stuck her head in.

"Oh, there you are," she said. "I just got back from a shoot, and Mrs. Hill said you were in the apartment. I went to look for you in your room, but Paige said she hadn't seen you since she got back an hour ago." She stopped. "Hey, that's an *amazing* dress!"

"Isn't it?" I said. I spun around once so she could see.

"Yeah," said Kerri. "Wow, where'd you get it?"

"Oh, Pia made it out of another dress I had," I said.

"That's really great, Pia," said Kerri.

"*Grazie*, thank you," said Pia.

"My other dress never got here, so I'm going to wear this to my meeting with Mr. Janelle tomorrow," I said.

"Oh, it's perfect," said Kerri. "Gosh, Pia, I still can't believe you made it."

"Hey," I said, "why don't we go back to my

room and see how it looks with those little black boots I got?"

"Okay," said Kerri.

As we went down the hall I realized that I was really excited now. My meeting with Mr. Janelle was less than a day away, but now I had the perfect thing to wear. It didn't matter that my mother hadn't sent the dress. I was beginning to feel like tomorrow could end up being a very big day for me after all.

CHAPTER 5

"Mr. Janelle will be here in just a moment," said the young sandy-haired man in jeans, T-shirt, and a blazer. "Come with me."

I followed him down the hall of the office building.

"You can wait in here," he said, opening a door to the right. "Please have a seat," he said, waving me inside.

"Thanks," I said. "I'll be fine."

He smiled and left, closing the door behind him. I looked around.

It was a large office with light gray carpeting and a big black desk with silver trim. I liked the sleek, high-tech style of it. To complete the look there were large wraparound windows. Because the office was on the thirty-ninth floor that meant that you got a truly incredible view from two sides. The sky was clear and blue, and the buildings outside looked like space-age building blocks laid out by a giant alien. I bet it looked great at night with the lights shining all over the city.

I always think New York looks best from way up high. You can't see the grime or hear the traffic, and everything looks more the way I always pictured New York would be before I moved here—all glittering and glamorous and exciting.

Against one wall of the office was a big couch covered in a deep blue material that I suddenly realized was denim. Opposite the couch were two black leather chairs with silver trim, and in the middle was a large black lacquer coffee table. Mounted on the wall behind the couch were several framed Janelle jeans advertisements.

"Sitting Pretty…with Janelle" said the first ad. It showed a model with curly blond hair sitting on a swing in a forest. Sunlight was streaming through the leaves making patterned shadows across the scene. The model's head was thrown back and she was laughing. There was a guy with dark red hair behind

her. He was also laughing. They both wore
Janelle jeans, and the girl had on a pink-and-
white checked shirt that was tied at the waist.
On her head was a floppy yellow straw hat
that probably had fallen off the second after
the picture was taken.

Another ad showed a model with long
chestnut braids with ribbons tied at the ends.
She wore Janelle jeans, of course, and a white
T-shirt with the sleeves rolled up. She was sitting in a tree with a basket of apples on the
branch next to her and a sprig of leaves
tucked into one of the ribbons on her braids.
She was looking out at the camera with a teas-
ing smile on her face. On the ground below
her, looking up at her and biting into an
apple, was a well-muscled guy with short
black hair. All he wore was a pair of worn
Janelle jeans with holes in the knees and work
boots with the laces undone. The caption read
"Back to Basics...with Janelle."

The third ad, which was directly over the
couch, said "Making a Splash...with Janelle."
It pictured a girl with tousled, wet shoulder-
length blond hair in a green-and-white polka-
dot bikini top and a pair of Janelle jeans that

were cut off so short that they looked almost like bikini bottoms. She was running along a wide beach with a dark-haired guy, also in cut-off Janelle jeans. The models were splashing each other with water and the drops sparkled in the air.

The blond girl looked very familiar to me now that I looked at her. In fact, I was almost positive she had been one of the models in the Supermodel contest, the one from Sweden. Karin…Karin…Karin something. Karin Anderson? That was it! Karin Anderson. Or was it her, after all? It was hard to tell, because of the water splashing around her face.

I moved around the coffee table, closer to the couch, and peered up at the picture. I just *had* to know if that was Karin. I mean, she wasn't even one of the finalists. Was it possible that she'd already done an ad for Janelle? I couldn't help feeling a bit jealous. I didn't know that Ford had signed Karin on as a model. But how else could she have ended up as a Janelle girl?

I stretched up on my toes to look at the picture, but I still couldn't get a good view of the model's face. Maybe if I just climbed up on the couch for a *moment*....

Unfortunately, that was the moment when the door opened and three people walked in. So there I was, standing on top of the denim couch in my long dress hiked up over my knees and black boots, while a woman and two men, one of whom, I knew, must be Maurice Janelle, stared at me.

I froze. I had no idea what to do. How was I going to get down from there without looking incredibly ridiculous? They must have thought I was nuts.

Then I remembered: sometimes if you act like you know what you're doing, other people will fall for it, too. So I hopped down from the couch to the floor with a smile, as if I did this sort of thing every day.

"Ta-da!" I said, waving my hands with a flourish.

To my relief one of the men broke into a huge smile. He was dressed in black with his dark hair slicked into a short ponytail.

"Ah, but this is *magnifique*, fantastic!" he said, clapping his hands and rubbing them together. "Ford has sent me a girl with some real energy. Some zest. Some *spirit*."

I glanced at the other man, who was dressed all in black also. His bleached white hair was cut very short and he wore perfectly round sunglasses. The sunglasses were so dark that I couldn't see his eyes. It didn't matter though, because as far as I could tell he was completely expressionless. Next to him, an auburn-haired woman wearing a green suit seemed less enthusiastic as well. In fact, she still looked a little surprised.

"*Bonjour, bonjour*, hello," the man with the ponytail said to me, extending his hand. "I am Maurice Janelle. It is truly a pleasure to meet such a lovely lady."

"Hi," I said with a grin as I shook his hand. "Cassandra. Cassandra Contiago. Nice to meet you."

"Here's our advertising director, Ms. Ann Bacon," he said. He waved in the direction of the woman in the suit. Then he nodded toward the other man. "And this gentleman over here is our photographer, Zane."

"Nice to meet you, Ms. Bacon," I said. "Mr. Zane."

"Not *Mr.* Zane," the photographer said. I waited for him to go on. Instead, he took a toothpick out of his pocket, put it into the corner of his mouth, and started to chew.

"Pardon me?" I said, confused.

"It's *Zane*," he told me, "just Zane."

"Zane is a genius, an *artiste*," said Janelle. He pointed to the couch. "Please, Cassandra, have a seat. Or, if you prefer, you may stand on the furniture." He burst into laughter again.

I was beginning to get a pretty good idea of how to impress Mr. Janelle.

"Thanks, I think I'll sit right here," I said, perching on the edge of the coffee table and smiling.

"*Ooo la la!* I love it!" said Mr. Janelle, laughing again. He sat down on the denim couch. He looked up at Ms. Bacon and Zane. "What do you think? Does this girl not have it?"

"The pictures Ford sent over of her were very nice," agreed Ms. Bacon. She sat in one of the chairs and crossed her legs in a businesslike manner.

"Ah, but I am not talking about her face," said Mr. Janelle. "Although, of course it is a very pretty one, we can see. I am speaking of her attitude, her *deportment*. Does she not have the 'Wild and Reckless' spirit?"

"'Wild and Reckless'?" I repeated.

"*Mais oui*, but of course," said Mr. Janelle.

"That's the new Janelle jeans ad campaign," explained Ms. Bacon. "'Wild and Reckless...with Janelle.'"

"Which I, *bien sur*, of course, came up with myself," said Mr. Janelle. He shook his head. "I wonder what I pay you people for sometimes." He turned to me. "So, Cassandra, please, tell me a bit about yourself, so that I may see if you really are the 'Wild and Reckless' Janelle girl I am looking for."

So, he wants wild and reckless, I thought. Okay, here goes.

"Well, I'm from Rio de Janeiro," I began. "Which is a *wild* city, as I'm sure you know, Mr. Janelle." He nodded his head, which gave me a second to think. I tried to remember the most reckless thing I'd ever done. "We've got these really high mountains in Rio, which are perfect for hang gliding off. You ride on the wind and come in for a landing on the beach."

"Hang gliding! *Oooo la la!*" Mr. Janelle

beamed. "So, you are a hang glider?"

"Sure," I said with a shrug.

Actually, I *had* hang glided. Once. Lots of people in Rio do it, so we decided to devote a special segment to it on *Qual o lance?*, my TV show. I didn't actually control the hang glider. That was done by a professional instructor. But I was strapped into it with him. The whole thing is on film. It was exciting, flying through the air with nothing between me and the ground. I don't know if I'd ever do it on my own, though. It doesn't seem very safe.

"Ah, so you are something of a daredevil, then," said Mr. Janelle.

"Absolutely," I told him. "Hang gliding, motorcycle racing, rock climbing…"

So I was stretching things a bit. But it was partially true. I mean I had been hang gliding that once. And I used to have a boyfriend in Rio who rode me around on the back of his motorcycle. The only one I hadn't done was rock climbing, but I knew what a rock was, didn't I? And climbing a few couldn't be that hard, could it? I was sure that if I *wanted* to rock climb, I *could* rock climb. I just hadn't gotten around to it yet, that's all.

And Mr. Janelle was *definitely* going for it. By the time I'd finished describing my "wild and reckless" hobbies, he was grinning from ear to ear.

"*Alors*, well," he said. He clapped his hands, sat back on the denim couch, and looked around happily. "It seems to me that we have found our next Janelle girl."

I felt a shiver of excitement go through me. I had the job! I could hardly believe it, it had all happened so fast.

Mr. Janelle turned to the woman in green. "Do you not agree, Ms. Bacon?"

"I told you, Mr. Janelle, I was willing to go with Cassandra from what we saw in her book," she said. "If you are happy with her, I'm more than pleased to go along with it."

"Ah, *c'est ridicule*, how absurd, her book!" he said, waving his hands. "What could that tell us? Only that she had a pretty face. I had to meet her myself to know for certain, to see the spirit."

Mr. Janelle turned to look at Zane, the photographer, who was still standing and chewing on his toothpick. He hadn't said a word since we'd been introduced.

"Well, Zane," said Mr. Janelle. "What says my *artiste?*"

Zane turned toward me. I smiled recklessly at him.

"Yes," he said, gnawing away, "I can work with her."

Well, I thought, that wasn't exactly enthusiastic. But apparently it was enough for Mr. Janelle.

"*Tres bien*, very well," he said. "It is set." He turned to me. "Unless you have any questions, Cassandra?"

"No," I said, shaking my head. I was just excited that I was going to be working for Mr. Janelle. Then I thought of something. "Actually, I do have one question."

"*Certainment*, of course, what is it?" said Mr. Janelle.

I pointed to the advertisement on the wall, the one with the blond girl on the beach. "Is that Karin Anderson?"

"Who?" said Mr. Janelle, looking up at the picture. "I'm sorry, I don't know who you mean."

"That's okay, never mind," I said, secretly

pleased to hear that Mr. Janelle hadn't ever heard of Karin Anderson.

"Well, then," he said, standing up from the denim couch and giving me a huge smile. "*Bienvenue*, a big welcome to the newest Janelle girl!"

CHAPTER 6

"Okay, Cassandra, look up, please," said Ricky, the makeup artist.

I raised my eyes, and he applied mascara to my lower lashes.

"Great," he said.

It was six in the morning the following Tuesday. I was sitting on a canvas chair with a towel draped over my shoulders in one of the location vans for the big Janelle shoot.

A car had picked me up at the apartment. From there it had been a forty-five-minute drive to the Coney Island Amusement Park, where the shoot was going to take place. That's one thing that's a pain about modeling—getting up early. Before coming to New York, I'd slept as late as I wanted. Now I was always getting up early for shoots. Photographers prefer the light early in the morning.

Also, when you're shooting at a location like an amusement park, it's a lot easier if you get there long before the place opens and gets crowded.

"Okay," said Ricky, finishing my eyes. "Now the lips."

I looked into the lighted mirror in front of me and stretched out my mouth so he could brush on some dark mocha lipstick.

I caught Ricky's eye in the mirror. He was about twenty-five and had short dark hair and a determined expression on his face.

"Should I blend?" I asked him.

He nodded. I pressed my lips together and rubbed them from side to side to smooth out the lipstick.

"All right," he said. "Now we'll just give you a light coat of powder to seal it all."

I watched in the mirror as he brushed powder all over my face.

"Okay," he said. "On to your hair."

Ricky was a makeup artist who did hair, too. Sometimes hair and makeup are done by different people.

"Now," said Ricky, studying me, "Mr. Janelle said he wants a dramatic look for you."

"Mr. Janelle?" I asked. "Is he going to be here?"

"Oh, yes," said Ricky. "Mr. Janelle is *always* at all his shoots."

Some clients, like Maurice Janelle, go to the shoots, and others leave everything up to the photographer. I hadn't thought about it before, but from what I had seen of Mr. Janelle, he was definitely the type who wanted to be involved.

Ricky brushed out my hair and squeezed a dab of gel onto his hands. Then he spread the gel evenly onto my hair and combed it straight back, away from my face.

"There," he said, spritzing on some hairspray. "Perfect."

I had to agree. I looked *good.* Something about having my dark hair slicked back set off the dramatic eye makeup and lipstick.

"Thanks," I said. "I like it."

"Good. Let's hope Mr. Janelle does, too," said Ricky. "He's very particular." Ricky took the towel off my shoulders and shook it out. "Okay, off to the other trailer for your clothes, Janelle girl. It's time for me to take care of the Janelle boy."

"The Janelle boy?" I repeated.

"Sure," said Ricky. "You know, the male model for this shoot."

"Oh, of course," I said, remembering that Janelle's ads always showed a girl and a guy together.

It's usually fun working with other models, especially guys. There's a certain chemistry that can happen between you that can make the shoot exciting. At least I knew the Janelle boy would be really cute. All the Janelle boys were. And that would definitely make the shoot more fun!

"The wardrobe van is to the left," said Rick. "Chloë, the stylist, will take care of you in there."

"Okay, Ricky," I said. "Thanks."

I was about to push open the door to the trailer when it opened by itself. Standing in front of me, in a black leather jacket, a white T-shirt, and black jeans, was Trevor Stone, the model I'd met at Ford the day I'd heard about the Janelle job.

"What are *you* doing here?" we said at the same time.

"What do you mean?" I asked. "I'm booked for this shoot."

"Well," said Trevor, "so am I."

"*Ta brincando!* You're kidding!" I said. "You mean Janelle was the big-name designer who was supposed to look at your book that day?"

"That's right," he said. "And I guess this was the big job you said you were up for." He grinned. "I told you we were both on the same schedule, Cassandra."

"Looks that way, doesn't it?" I said, grinning back. I pushed past him and turned left, toward the wardrobe van. "See you on the set, Trevor."

"Yeah, okay," he said, heading into the makeup van. "Catch you later."

I couldn't believe it. The Janelle boy had turned out to be Trevor! No doubt about it, this shoot was going to be fun! Not only was Trevor gorgeous, but we also seemed to hit it off pretty well. In fact, I was beginning to think he might be interested in me. I have a sixth sense about these things. I can always tell when a guy likes me. And I was definitely getting signals from Trevor.

I pulled open the door to the wardrobe van. Inside I found the stylist. She was a pretty woman with dark blond hair, wearing a red-and-white striped T-shirt and black leggings. She was using a small portable steamer to smooth out the wrinkles in a pair of Janelle jeans.

"Hi," she said. "You must be Cassandra. I'm Chloë."

"Hi," I said. "So what do I wear?"

"Well, to start, these are just about ready for you," she said, handing me the jeans. "And I thought we'd try them with this first." She picked up a red cotton tank top with spaghetti straps.

"Great," I answered, taking the clothes from her. I pulled off my own black cotton minidress, stepped into the jeans, and carefully eased the tank top over my hair and make-up.

"Great," she said, surveying me. "Now try these." She gave me a pair of high-heeled, black ankle boots with buckles.

"Perfect," she said with a smile. "Janelle will love it." Then she paused. "At least, I hope so, because if he doesn't, we're all sure to hear about it. Why don't you go out and let him have a look? I think he and the photographer are setting up over by the bumper-car ride."

Outside the van, I looked around. There was something odd about seeing an amusement park empty. The rides were motionless, the food stands boarded up, and the game areas gated over. A huge white wooden roller-coaster track was silhouetted against the sky. I shivered a little. I've always liked amusement parks, but I hadn't been on a roller coaster since I was eight. That was when my older brother took me on a giant one and nearly scared me to death. I looked at this one and thought about how the cars would be filled with screaming people in a few short hours.

I spotted Maurice Janelle, Zane, Ms. Bacon, and two other people over by the bumper cars. Mr. Janelle was talking and waving his hands in the air. Ms. Bacon was nodding. Zane was peering through the lens of a camera, ignoring everyone around him. The two other people were running around adjusting lights and reflectors. One was a short, heavyset man with a long ponytail and a beard—he was wearing a walkie-talkie on his belt. The other was a tall, thin woman with brown hair and glasses. I decided they were Zane's assistants. I also noticed an old man in coveralls sitting in the control booth of the bumper car ride. His head was tilted back and his eyes were closed.

When Mr. Janelle saw me, his face lit up.

"Ah, here she is," he said. "Our Janelle girl. You look marvelous, positively *magnifique!*" He looked around a moment. "And where is my Janelle boy?"

The man with the beard picked up his walkie-talkie.

"Janelle wants Trevor on the set," he said.

"*Alors*, meanwhile, let me start with you, Cassandra." Mr. Janelle took me by the hand and led me up the ramp to the ride's entrance. "Let us put you in one of these contraptions and see how it works."

He banged on the glass of the control booth, and the old man jolted awake.

"Keep alert, you!" yelled Janelle. "I'm not paying you to take a nap."

The old man muttered, sat up straight, and pulled a lever. The headlights of the bumper cars lit up, and little sparks began to fly from the tops of their antennas. Wow, I thought, how fun! It looks like we're actually going to get to ride on these.

Ricky, Chloë, and Trevor came toward us.

Trevor was wearing a black T-shirt with the sleeves cut off, black boots, and, of course, Janelle jeans.

"Ah, *en fin*, finally!" said Janelle. "My Janelle boy is here. Have you met our lovely Janelle girl?"

"Oh yeah," said Trevor, giving me a little wink. "We've met."

"Good," said Janelle. "Then we begin. Janelle girl, why don't we put you in that blue car over there, and Janelle boy, you take the red one beside it."

Trevor and I stepped into the bumper-car track area and made our way across it to the two cars.

"Well," said Trevor, sliding into place behind the wheel of his red car and glancing at me, "I guess I should warn you now, I can be a pretty wild driver." He gave me a devilish grin.

"Hey," I said, settling into my own blue car and adjusting the seat belt, "you don't realize who you're talking to. I'm from Rio. We drive on the sidewalks and don't stop for red lights. Or anything."

"Well, excuse me," joked Trevor. "I guess I'd better watch out, huh, Rio?"

"That's right, Michigan," I said, flashing him a smile.

Ricky gave us quick touch-ups on our hair and makeup, and Chloë straightened out the wrinkles in our clothes.

"Okay?" she said, looking at Mr. Janelle, who had gone to stand by Zane.

"*Magnifique!* Wonderful!" beamed Mr. Janelle.

"But we can't even see the jeans," complained Ms. Bacon.

"Ah, who cares about the jeans?" said Janelle. "It is the *spirit* of the jeans I wish to capture."

I shook my head. That Maurice Janelle was a strange one.

Mr. Janelle looked at Zane. "My *artiste*, you are ready?"

Zane stepped over the railing of the trackway and crouched down with his camera.

Mr. Janelle clapped his hands. "*Alors*, all right, now we begin."

Mr. Janelle wanted us to start by driving our cars around the track. He had one of the assistants put an *X* in masking tape on the floor of the track so we'd know exactly when we were passing the spot where Zane would be snapping the picture.

"And *s'il vous plait*, please," Mr. Janelle added, "enjoy, have fun. Show me that 'Wild and Reckless' spirit of the Janelle girl and boy."

"Okay, Rio," said Trevor, starting his car. "Don't say I didn't warn you!"

"Just worry about yourself, Michigan," I shot back.

Trevor took off down the track, with me close behind him. As we flew around the track, smashing into the other cars, I tried to overtake him. But somehow, he kept slipping away. On top of trying to catch up with him, I had to remember to turn my face toward the camera every time I drove over the *X* on the floor.

"You're a pretty big talker, Rio!" Trevor called, his car scuttling off between two others.

"Oh, yeah?" I said, seeing an opening in the center of the trackway. I made a sharp left and cut off his car, right at the point where the *X* was.

"Take that, Michigan!" I called, laughing.

A moment later I felt a tremendous bump from the left side. Trevor had wedged my car into a corner.

"Gotcha!" he said.

"*Magnifique*, beautiful!" called Mr. Janelle, as Zane's camera clicked away. "This is the spirit I am looking for."

I managed to free my car, and Trevor and I continued to chase each other around the track, screaming and laughing as Mr. Janelle shouted directions and Zane shot away with his camera. I had never had so much fun on a shoot. Whenever Ricky or Chloë stopped us to fix our hair, makeup, or clothes, I couldn't wait to get started again.

And Trevor seemed to be enjoying himself as much as I was. He took the turns at top speed, bumping and crashing whatever cars were in his way, including mine.

Finally, after several rolls of film, Mr. Janelle told us to stop.

"*Fantastique*, marvelous!" he beamed. "And now, we move to the roller coaster."

CHAPTER 7

I gulped. My smile must have looked a little shaky because Trevor gave me a funny look. Then he grinned.

"What's the matter, Rio?" asked Trevor. "You're not chicken, are you?"

"No, no," I lied. "I love roller coasters. They're great."

But I was nervous. I knew it didn't make sense. I'd done more daring things than ride a roller coaster. But the memory of that time with my brother was too strong. Just thinking about it made me feel like a little girl again.

Still, the last thing I wanted was for Trevor, or for that matter, Mr. Janelle, to know how I was feeling. After all, I was supposed to be the "Wild and Reckless" Janelle girl. So I put on my most easygoing smile.

77

"Okay," I said, trying to sound enthusiastic. "The roller coaster—let me at it."

Mr. Janelle wanted us to change clothes and have our hair and makeup touched up first, so we went back to the location vans. For these shots, Trevor was going to wear a white sleeveless muscle shirt with his Janelle jeans, and I had a black *bustier* with mine.

A few minutes later, we were in front of the enormous white wooden track of the roller coaster. I took deep breaths trying to slow down my pounding heart.

Trevor grinned at me as the old man from the bumper cars took his place in the control booth of the roller coaster. "Sure you're up to it, Rio?"

I raised an eyebrow. "If you are, Michigan."

Mr. Janelle told us to sit in the second car of the roller coaster. Ms. Bacon shook her head again sadly. I knew she was thinking that no one would be able to see the jeans in these shots either. But she didn't say anything. Trevor and I settled in place and pulled the safety bar across our laps as Mr. Janelle and Zane climbed into the first car. They both turned to face us.

"*Alors*, now," said Mr. Janelle, "I wish to

see here the same wonderful spirit from my Janelle girl and boy here as you showed before!"

Mr. Janelle gave the signal to the old man in the booth, and the roller coaster jerked into motion. Zane began snapping photos. I gripped the safety bar, hoping Trevor wouldn't notice how white my knuckles were turning as we climbed slowly to the top of the first hill.

Finally, we were all the way up. I could see that this hill was the smallest one, but as we teetered at the top I could feel my palms sweating. I wished I could close my eyes, but I knew that was impossible, since Zane was still shooting us with his camera. I took a deep breath and let it out.

The next thing I knew, we were racing down the hill. My heart felt like it was in my throat, and everything around me was one big blur. I could hear Trevor laughing gleefully next to me and Mr. Janelle yelling directions in front of me.

A few moments later, the first descent was over. I could feel my heart pounding as we began to climb again, the wheels of the cars clicking over the rails.

"Wow, is this great or what, Rio?" asked Trevor, turning to look at me.

"Yeah," I said. I was feeling a little sick. "Wonderful."

"*Fantastique!* Marvelous!" shouted Mr. Janelle. He grinned wildly at us as Zane snapped away with the camera. "These shots will be the best, for sure."

As the ride went on, I tried to look like I was having fun. I knew it was important to have just the right expression on my face, especially since Mr. Janelle seemed so into these roller-coaster shots. There was a pretty good chance he might want to use one of them for the advertisement.

Amazingly enough, as the ride went on, I did get used to it. It helped if I took a deep breath at the top of each hill and let it out as we went down.

Then I saw the last hill, the largest one of the ride, looming up ahead. It was huge, much bigger than any of the others.

"*Alors*, all right," boomed Mr. Janelle, "now let's see some of that 'Wild and Reckless' spirit from my Janelle girl and boy."

As we climbed to the top, Trevor reached out and put his arm around me.

"Ah, *tres bien*, this I like very much," shouted Janelle.

I had to agree. Even though my heart was racing, it felt great to have Trevor's arm around me. I felt much safer. At least I wasn't going to die alone. Trevor gave my shoulder a little squeeze.

"How you doing, Rio?" he asked. "Okay?"

"Sure, great," I said. We were almost at the top, and I wasn't about to let him see how nervous I was. To show him that I was okay, I let go of the safety bar for a moment.

"Hey, great idea!" said Trevor, his eyes twinkling.

"What?" I asked.

"This," he said. He reached out, grabbed both of my hands in his, and raised them up in the air just as the roller coaster began its dive.

As we hurtled down the hill, I felt my stomach rise up into my throat. I was sure that I was about to bounce out of the car. I could hardly breathe. Trevor was holding my arms above my head. I opened my mouth to scream, but no sound came out.

Then, suddenly, there was a giant shriek. It was me! I could hear Trevor screaming and laughing beside me. I leaned into him and felt him squeeze my hands. I felt like I was flying. Finally, it was all over. The roller coaster glided to a stop. I gulped for air.

"*Fantastique! Fantastique!*" Mr. Janelle was yelling excitedly. A lot of his hair had come out of its ponytail and was sticking out from the sides of his head.

"*Puxa!*" I said, still trying to catch my breath. "Wow!"

"Incredible!" said Trevor, still laughing.

Zane put down his camera. He was looking a little green.

"Perfect, perfect," said Janelle. He grinned wildly, his face shining. "I have my 'Wild and Reckless' photo, to be sure. *Merci*, thank you both, my Janelle girl and boy, for an excellent day's work."

Trevor and I climbed out of the car and headed back toward the trailers. My legs wobbled a little beneath me.

"Wow," said Trevor, "that was great. It reminded me of snowmobiling."

"Snowmobiling?" I said.

"Sure," he said. "My friends and I used to do it in Michigan."

"I guess it must be like jet-skiing," I said. "We do that on the beach in Rio."

"Ah, it's not the same without the snow," said Trevor.

"Well, excuse me," I joked, "but we don't happen to have any snow in Rio."

"Oh, that's right," said Trevor. He shook his head. "No snow, huh? Winter sports are the greatest. Snowmobiling, snowboarding, ice skating. You don't know what you're missing, Rio."

"Brrrrr, sounds cold to me," I said.

"Not if you've got someone with you to keep you warm," he said.

I smiled. "Oh, really?" I asked.

"Hey, I've got an idea," he said. "How'd you like to check out some winter fun right now, Rio?"

"What do you mean?" I asked.

"Ice skating," he said.

"Correct me if I'm wrong," I said. "I mean, I've never been ice skating or anything, but isn't it kind of hard to find ice in the summer?"

"No problem," he said. "I know a great indoor rink right in the city."

"Okay," I said. "Sounds fun."

My sixth sense had been right. Trevor *was* interested in me! Maybe he hadn't noticed how scared I'd been, after all. This was turning into some day. First a shoot for Janelle jeans, and now a date with Trevor—and a chance to try ice skating, too.

CHAPTER 8

"There's really an ice skating rink in here?" I asked as Trevor and I walked into the lobby of a huge steel-and-glass building. "It looks like an office building to me."

"It is," said Trevor. "I mean, it's mostly businesses. But there's a rink on the top floor. Sometimes people from the offices below even come up on their lunch breaks. It's funny to see them skating around in their business suits."

"So," I said as we stepped into the elevator, "it sounds like you come here often."

"Twice a week," said Trevor. "Tuesdays and Thursdays."

That's strange, I thought. I mean, twice a week was *really* often. And why always Tuesdays and Thursdays? But I didn't say anything. After all, I knew absolutely nothing about ice skating. Maybe there was a reason, although I couldn't imagine what.

The elevator opened on the top floor, and we stepped into a hallway with doors on both sides. The floor was covered with a thick black rubber mat.

"So where's the ice?" I asked.

"Patience, Rio," said Trevor. "You'll see it. The rink's through that door at the end of the hall."

As we started down the hall, I heard a booming voice behind us.

"Yo! Stone!"

Trevor stopped, and we turned. A big guy with short dark hair was coming down the hall toward us. He had big black skates with white laces and a blue-and-white jersey with the number seventy-five and the word *Blades* on it. In his hand was a blue helmet.

"Yo, Stone," the guy said again. "What's happening?"

"Hey, McKinnon!" said Trevor. The two of them high-fived.

"Glad to see you made it, pretty boy," cracked McKinnon. "Coach said you miss one more practice this month and you're out."

Practice, I thought. What's he talking about?

"Hey, man, I can't help it if I've got to earn a living," said Trevor.

McKinnon looked at me and grinned. "Looks like you brought your own cheering section."

"Yeah, this is Cassandra," said Trevor. "She's from Brazil, so it's her first time at a rink. I thought she might get a kick out of watching."

"Watching?" I repeated.

"Yeah," said Trevor. "Hockey practice. I'm in a league here in New York. Our team's the Blades, and we practice Tuesdays and Thursdays."

"That's right," said McKinnon. "We've got a good chance of winning the league cup this year, too, thanks to our star center over here." He looked at Trevor. "Hey, you better get suited up and out on the ice, guy."

"Sure," said Trevor. "Let me just show Cassandra where she can sit first."

I had to admit, I was kind of surprised. I'd been pretty sure that Trevor had been talking about taking me ice skating. Now it sounded like he'd only invited me to watch his practice. I guessed I'd misunderstood. But now that I thought about it, maybe it was better not to let Trevor see me my first time on skates.

Trevor and I walked through the door at the end of the hall and into a large, high-ceilinged room with several sets of wooden bleachers overlooking a large oval ice-skating rink. Several guys in blue Blades jerseys and helmets were already on the ice, passing a puck around with hockey sticks. An older man in a blue parka, who must have been the coach, was blowing a whistle in the center of the rink.

"*Puxa!* Wow!" I said, as the cool air hit my bare legs. "It's freezing in here!"

"Oh, yeah," said Trevor, looking at my black minidress. "You might get kind of cold in that. Here, I'll give you my jacket."

Trevor settled me into a seat on the bleachers and handed me his black leather jacket.

"I'd better go get changed," he said. "See you later, Rio."

As I sat in the bleachers waiting, I suddenly remembered Mrs. Hill. She was expecting me back at the apartment. It was pretty silly, but we were supposed to let her know anytime we went anywhere after a shoot. I looked around. If there was a pay phone nearby, I'd give her a call.

I spotted one against the far wall. But when I reached into my bag and took out my purse, I discovered that I didn't have any change. Oh well, I'd just have to explain it to her when I got home. How long could hockey practice take, anyway?

"A lot longer than I imagined" turned out to be the answer. First the coach had them all skate around the edge of the rink really fast, switching directions whenever he blew his whistle. Then they had to pair off and pass the puck back and forth while skating up and down the rink. And then came drill after drill after drill. I sat there shivering in my minidress and Trevor's jacket trying to keep my eyes on him on the ice. It was hard because, with his blue jersey and helmet on, he looked like all the other guys on the rink.

One thing I did notice, though, was how rough the sport was. The players were constantly knocking each other down on the ice and smashing each other against the side of the rink. It looked like it would be pretty easy to be hit by a stick or the puck. In fact, it was a strange hobby for a model to have. One bad scar and Trevor could be out of work for good. I was surprised that the Fords let him play.

After what seemed like ages, the practice was over. Trevor and the others skated to the edge of the ice and stepped off onto the rubber matting. Trevor and McKinnon made their way over to me.

"So, what did you think, Rio?" asked Trevor, sitting beside me.

"Pretty wild and reckless," I joked.

"Yeah," said Trevor, grinning. "It's a rough sport."

"Whew," said McKinnon, pulling off his helmet, "I'm beat."

"You?" said Trevor. "I've been up since dawn."

"Okay, you win," said McKinnon. He picked his helmet up. "See you in the locker room, Stone. Nice meeting you, Cassandra."

"Bye," I said. I turned to Trevor. "So, maybe after you change we could go get a bite to eat or something."

"Sorry, Rio, but I'm exhausted," he said. "All I want to do right now is get home and lie down."

"Oh," I said. "Okay, sure."

But I was kind of disappointed. I had been so sure that Trevor was interested in me. I'd hoped that somehow this was going to turn into more of a real date.

"Give me your number. I'll call you sometime," said Trevor.

"Sure," I said.

I reached into my bag and found a pen.

"I don't have anything to write on," I said.

Trevor held out his hand. "Just write it here."

"You sure?" I asked him.

"Yeah, go ahead," he said. "I do it all the time."

"Okay," I said. I leaned over his hand and wrote on his palm:

555-3643—RIO.

A little while later, I let myself in the apartment with my key. Naira was sitting on the living room floor with her appointment book and index cards spread around her.

She looked up through her dark curls when I came in.

"Hey, Cassandra, I'd get right in the kitchen and let Mrs. Hill know I was home if I were you," she said. "She's pretty upset."

Mrs. Hill must have heard me come in, because at that moment she came through the kitchen door.

"Cassandra! Do you realize what time it is?" she said.

"Oh, I'm sorry I'm late," I said. I dropped my bag by the hall table where she usually put our mail.

"Late?" she repeated. "Cassandra, we are not talking about a matter of minutes here, or even an hour. Ford told me your shoot ended almost three hours ago!"

"I said I was sorry," I said, sighing.

I glanced at Naira, but she was looking down at her appointment book. Boy, I thought, does Mrs. Hill really have to yell at me in front of Naira? She's treating me like a baby.

Mrs. Hill shook her head. "Cassandra, I really think you need to sit down and take a good look at your attitude lately. I don't know if you realize how much your actions affect other people. What was I supposed to think when you didn't show up or call after your shoot? As far as I was concerned, it was very possible that something dreadful had happened to you. I am responsible for all of you. What would you want me to tell your mother?"

"Not that my mother would care," I muttered under my breath. Then I sighed. "All right, I know, I know," I said. "So I didn't follow the *rules*. I'm sorry. I'm sorry. What else do you want me to say?"

Mrs. Hill looked at me for a long moment. "One day, you may realize that these rules are for your own protection, Cassandra," she said. "I just hope you don't have to learn it the hard way."

She turned and walked back into the kitchen.

"You know," said Naira quietly, "one simple phone call and you could have avoided all this, Cassandra."

"Excuse me for saying so, Naira," I said, "but nobody asked you."

"Just trying to help," said Naira.

"Well, thanks but no thanks," I said.

I reached for my bag on the mail table. There was a package with my name on it. It had been overnight expressed from Brazil. It had to be the dress from my mother.

Well, I thought, exasperated, that was so nice of her to send it a week late. A lot of good it does me now. But it was just so typical of her. Like I said, she's not the kind of person anyone can depend on.

CHAPTER 9

"Cass, Cass, wake up!" said Kerri, shaking my shoulder.

"Aaahhh, *depois*, later," I said. I put my head under the pillow.

Kerri shook me again.

"Come on, Cass, get up!" she said.

I peeked out from under my pillow. Paige's bed across the room was empty. As usual it was neatly made, with the ruffles of her pink-and-white checked bedspread lined up perfectly and her tattered stuffed rabbit sitting on her pillow. I looked at my own side of the room, the piles of makeup and jewelry on my dresser, the clothes thrown on the floor.

"What time is it?" I asked.

"Ten after nine," said Kerri.

I groaned. It was one of the few mornings I didn't have to get up for a booking, a test, or a go-see, and I'd planned on sleeping until at least eleven.

"Listen," said Kerri, "I have exciting news. It's about Janelle."

I looked at her. "Did you say Janelle?"

"That's right," she said. "Jill Murray just called from Ford to say that Mr. Janelle loved the pictures you did for him."

"*Puxa!* Wow!" I said, sitting up in bed. "You mean he's going to use them?"

"Not only that," said Kerri, "but he liked them so much that he's throwing a big party tomorrow at the Vault to unveil his new ads. All the Ford models are invited."

"Oh, Kerri, that's great," I said, rubbing my eyes and yawning. "Can I go back to sleep now?"

"No way. We've got to figure out what to wear," said Kerri. "After all, the party's tomorrow and I've never been to the Vault before."

The Vault was the hottest new club in New York. It was called the Vault because it was in a building that had once been a bank. I'd never been there either, but I'd read all about it in *Buzz*, a chic New York gossip newspaper. *Buzz* has a column called "Hip and Happening," all about the hottest parties and events. There were always pictures of famous and cool people partying at the Vault.

Since the party was for the "Wild and Reckless" ads, I knew Trevor would be there, too. Actually, I was kind of surprised that a whole day had gone by since the Janelle shoot and our "date" without his calling. I'd kind of started wondering when we would get together again. Now I knew I'd see him at the party.

"Let's go shopping and get something new," said Kerri.

How could she have so much energy so early in the morning? I wondered. "Actually, I think I know what to wear," I said, thinking of the package that had arrived on Tuesday. "My mother sent the maroon dress I told you about."

"Oh, that's great," said Kerri. "Can I see it?"

"Sure," I said. "It's in the closet, on the left."

Kerri walked over to the closet. I closed my eyes and heard her sliding hangers along the metal rod.

"Oh, here it is," she said. "Wow, Cass, it's

cool. Really different, you know? And there's no way anyone else will have one like it."

"Mmmm...." I said, already starting to drift back to sleep.

"Hey," she said suddenly, "what are you doing? You can't go back to sleep! You've got to get up!"

"Why?" I said, my eyes still closed.

"To go shopping," said Kerri.

I opened my eyes and looked at her. "I told you, I'm wearing the maroon dress."

"Yeah, but *I* still don't have anything for the party," said Kerri. "Aren't you going to help me look?"

I sighed. "Oh, I don't know, Kerri. I'm tired. Maybe you should just go alone."

"I *can't*," Kerri wailed. "I mean, I really, *really* need your advice, Cass," she added more softly.

"Sorry," I said as I rolled over. "I don't feel like getting up yet. Check back with me in a couple hours."

"I have a go-see in a couple of hours," said Kerri. "Come on, Cass, please? Didn't I help you figure out what to wear for the Janelle interview? And I went shopping with you for those black boots. That's what friends are for."

I thought about it a moment. I guessed Kerri was right. It was funny, though. I hadn't given it a second thought when she'd helped me with my fashion crisis. It was only now that I realized she'd done me a favor.

"Okay, Kerri," I said, throwing back the covers. "Let's get out there and hit the stores."

"Thank you," I said as the uniformed driver opened the door to the long black limousine.

I smoothed down my long maroon dress and slid into the car. Inside were Maurice Janelle, Zane, and Trevor. I sat beside Trevor, facing Mr. Janelle and Zane.

It was the night of the big party at the Vault. Kerri and the others were already at the party, but Mr. Janelle had decided that the four of us should arrive a little late, so we could be sure to make a big entrance.

Trevor was dressed in a formal tuxedo jacket and pants with a white T-shirt.

"Hey, what's happening, Rio?" he said. He grinned as I took my seat.

"Hey, Michigan," I said. I flashed him a smile. Trevor hadn't called me yet, but I figured it was because he'd known he'd see me at the party anyway.

"Ah, *quelle jolie!* How beautiful you look, my Janelle girl," said Mr. Janelle. He turned to Zane. "Is she not the picture of loveliness?"

Zane nodded. Then he took a toothpick from the pocket of his white jacket, stuck it in the corner of his mouth, and started to gnaw on it like a dog with a bone.

"Tonight, you will see, my Janelle girl and boy, the vision that this *artiste,*" Mr. Janelle said, nodding toward Zane, "that this brilliant *artiste* has created. I predict that the 'Wild and Reckless' campaign will be a tremendous success."

Zane continued to chew on his toothpick and gazed blankly out of the smoked window of the limo. I caught Trevor's eye, and he smiled. He looked as happy as I was feeling. It was funny, I hadn't thought of it this way until now, but the Janelle ads would probably be a big boost to his career, too. But I was pretty sure I detected something more in his smile, as well. Something special that was meant just for me.

A few minutes later we arrived in front of the Vault. The driver opened the door, and I was amazed to see a crowd of people outside.

There was a flurry of camera flashes as Mr. Janelle stepped out. Then Trevor got out and offered me his hand. I took it and slid out of the car.

As soon as Trevor and I were out on the sidewalk, the cameras started to flash even faster. The light was nearly blinding, and I held tight to Trevor's hand. With Mr. Janelle in front of us and Zane behind us, we made our way through the crowd to the door to the Vault. Two huge-muscled doormen in leather jackets moved aside and we walked in.

Inside the club it was even more crowded than on the street. As I looked around, I realized that Mr. Janelle must have invited everyone who was anyone to this party. I recognized several famous Ford models, as well as some people who regularly appeared in the "Hip and Happening" column of *Buzz*.

The Vault itself was amazing. Even though it had been turned into a club, most of the original stuff from when it had been a bank was still there. There was a huge clock against one wall with the words "Time to Save" written across its face, and a row of tellers' windows below it that had been made into a bar.

The dance floor to my right was centered around what must have been the bank's vault. Its huge, round metal door stood open, reflecting the flashing colored lights from the ceiling. Around it, a crowd of people bounced and swayed to the rhythm of the blasting dance music.

But without a doubt the most amazing thing in the whole place was the enormous photograph that covered one entire wall. It was of Trevor and me.

"*Puxa!*" I said, looking at it. "Wow!"

Mr. Janelle leaned toward me. "Is it not *magnifique?* Truly a work of art!"

"It's incredible," I said.

I looked at Trevor. He was gazing up at the photograph, his mouth open.

"What do you think, Michigan?" I said. "We make a pretty good team, huh?"

But Trevor didn't seem to hear me. He just kept staring up at the picture.

And I could see why. It was definitely amazing to see a picture of yourself that big. The photograph was one of the shots from the roller coaster, on that last big hill. In it Trevor had his arm around me as he held my hands up in the air. Our mouths were both open, we were leaning into each other, our hair flying out behind us. The caption read "Wild and Reckless...with Janelle."

The next thing I knew Kerri and Pia came rushing up to me. "Oh, Cass," said Kerri, throwing her arms around my neck. "I'm so happy for you."

"*Si, congratulazioni!*" said Pia.

"Thanks," I said, breaking into a huge smile.

"You look great," said Kerri, standing back to look at my outfit.

"So do you," I said. "Both of you."

It was true. The body-hugging pale yellow dress Kerri and I had picked out for her the day before made the gold highlights in her hair stand out. And Pia looked great with her short hair slicked forward in little curls— wearing a minidress she'd made from a man's tuxedo jacket.

"So, this is the famous Mr. Michigan, huh?" said Kerri in a low voice. She nodded her head toward Trevor, who was talking to a short, balding man with black square-framed glasses. On his shoulder was a large rectangular bag.

"That's right," I said. I looked at Trevor,

trying to get his attention, but he was too involved in his conversation. "I'll introduce you guys later."

Just then, I saw Jill Murray making her way through the crowd toward us.

"Hello, girls," she said. "Congratulations, Cassandra."

"Thanks," I said, smiling happily.

"It's going to look great in your book," she said. She nodded toward the photo on the wall. "Too bad we can't fit that one in," she joked.

We all laughed.

"Kerri and Pia, excuse me while I take Cassandra away from you for a few moments," said Jill. "Eileen and Jerry want to offer their congratulations."

"*Prego*," said Pia. "Go ahead."

"Sure," said Kerri. "We'll catch you later, Cass."

As Jill and I made our way through the crowd, I straightened my dress and smoothed back my hair.

We found Eileen and Jerry seated at a table near the dance floor. Eileen was wearing a cream-colored satin pantsuit, and Jerry had on his usual dark suit and tie. And sitting with them were Kimi Yardley and Laila, two of Ford's hottest supermodels. Kimi had on a multicolored sheer blouse over a black camisole top with black pants. Laila was wearing a long-sleeved white minidress with circle cutouts on the sleeves that showed off her dark skin. I couldn't believe it. Kimi and Laila were two of my favorite models.

Eileen stood up.

"Cassandra, dear," she said, taking my hand, "Jerry and I just wanted to give you our best wishes. The Janelle ad is really very striking."

"Yeah," said Kimi. "It's a great picture."

Laila squinted at me. "Where else have I seen your work?"

"Oh, I don't know," I said, waving my hand in the air. "You know, around." I wasn't about to tell her that before this my biggest ad campaign had been as Miss *Saude* Soda.

"And I'm sure you'll continue to see her around," said Jill. "This ad's a real winner."

"Yes, very nice work," said Jerry. "Thanks for bringing her over, Jill."

As we walked away from the table, I felt like I was about to burst with happiness. Not only had the Fords seemed impressed with the ad, but now two of the world's most famous models actually knew who *I* was.

"Well, I'll leave you to enjoy yourself, Cassandra," said Jill, winking at me. "After all, this is your big night."

That's right, I thought, and Trevor's, too. Which was why I should go back and find him. After all, it would be a good idea for the Janelle girl and the Janelle boy to be seen together tonight. Not that I exactly *minded* spending time with Trevor, I thought, remembering how cute he'd looked in his tuxedo jacket.

As I walked by the dance floor, I saw Naira and Pia dancing. Naira looked exotic in her sheer purple palazzo pants and a black and gold tapestry vest, her dark curls threaded with thin gold ribbons. Pia beckoned me to join them, but I waved and shook my head no. I wanted to find Trevor.

But he wasn't where he'd been standing before. I looked around, but I couldn't spot him anywhere. I did see Zane standing in the crowd by the bar, gnawing away on a toothpick. I hoped that at least it was a different toothpick from the one he'd started out with.

"Hi," I said, walking up to him. "Have you seen Trevor anywhere?"

Zane didn't even turn his head to look at me. He just continued chewing and shook his head.

"Okay, well, thanks anyway," I said, sighing. I was getting a little tired of Zane's silent act.

Then I spotted Trevor myself, across the room. He was standing in a crowd of people, talking to someone. By the way he was leaning over, I could tell it was someone who was shorter than he was. Probably that little man in the glasses he had been talking to before, I thought. I headed over in his direction. I wondered who that guy was. If Trevor was spending so much time with him, maybe he was someone important. His bag had looked like it could have been a camera bag. Maybe he was a photographer.

As I got to the other side of the room, I realized that Trevor wasn't talking to the guy in the glasses after all. In fact, he wasn't talking to any guy. The person standing opposite him, gazing up at him, was a girl. A very pretty girl with long silky black hair, wearing a white minidress with red polka dots. The dress reminded me of Minnie Mouse.

I veered away and began walking in another direction. Not that it was any big deal that Trevor was talking to a girl. I mean, it wasn't as if we'd come to the party as dates or anything. I just didn't feel like walking over there while he was talking to her. Why not wait until later, when I could have him all to myself?

CHAPTER 10

I spotted Paige, her boyfriend Jordan, and Katerina sitting at the end of a long, curved black couch against the wall. Paige was adorable as usual in her blue crushed velvet baby-doll dress, with her red curls spilling down her back.

Paige and Jordan are disgustingly cute together, like two little kids who are best friends. They're always laughing and gazing into one another's eyes. Tonight Jordan, who has wavy dark brown hair and green eyes, was wearing a deep green sweater and dark jeans. He and Paige were leaning forward, listening to something Katerina was saying.

Katerina's hair was twisted into a topknot with light brown curls falling onto her forehead. She was wearing a simple black dress with a deep scooped back. As usual, she was sitting up very straight. Paige had told me that Katerina used to be a ballerina or something back in Russia, so I guess that's where she gets her unbelievable posture.

Katerina looked a little different tonight, though. I tried to figure out what it was as I walked toward them. Then I realized that it was the look on her face. Instead of sitting silently with her usual distant gaze, she was leaning toward Paige and Jordan and talking, waving her hands. She looked almost upset, but she must have been telling quite a story, judging by the way Paige and Jordan were listening.

As I reached them, Katerina stopped talking and folded her hands in her lap.

"Oh, Cassandra, hi!" said Paige, smiling sweetly at me. "I've been looking for you. I wanted to tell you how great I think your picture is."

"*Da*, yes," said Katerina quietly, looking down at her hands. "Many congratulations to you."

"So," said Jordan, "I guess this jeans ad is a pretty big deal, huh?"

"Yeah," I said. "At least, I hope so."

Just then I saw Trevor walking back across the room.

"Um, I'll see you guys later, okay?" I said. "I have to go."

"Okay, but you should meet us back here pretty soon," said Paige, looking at her watch. "The cars are going to be here to take us back to the apartment in twenty minutes."

I sighed. Paige was as bad as Naira. Mrs. Hill had arranged for us all to be picked up at eleven-thirty, so we could be back by midnight. Why couldn't she forget about the rules for just one night?

I found Trevor near the bar.

"Hey, Rio," he said, grinning. "Some party, huh?"

"Yeah," I said, "if you like this sort of thing."

He looked at me. "What do you mean?"

"Oh, you know," I said. "Hot clubs, celebrities, chic clothes…" I tried to keep a straight face. "…giant pictures of yourself. What a bore."

Trevor caught my eye, and we both burst out laughing.

"Yeah, I guess this is pretty good for both of us," said Trevor.

Just then, Mr. Janelle walked over to us.

"Ah, my *magnifiques* Janelle girl and boy!" he gushed. "I have just come to say *adieu*, farewell."

"You mean you're going?" I asked.

"Yes," he said. "I must get my rest, for tomorrow I must begin to come up with the next brilliant idea for a Janelle jeans advertisement. I am thinking perhaps of 'Roughing It…with Janelle.'"

"Oh," I said.

It hadn't occurred to me that there would be another ad after this one, with a new Janelle girl and boy. But I guessed it made sense. When Mr. Janelle had gone, Trevor looked over my shoulder.

"Excellent!" he said, his face lighting up. "Ryan's here!"

"Ryan?" I repeated, turning to follow his gaze. When I saw who he was looking at, I could hardly believe my eyes. There, standing by the bar, were Ryan Goode and Derek Sinclair, the actors.

"You mean you know him?" I asked.

Ryan Goode had been a child star, and then a teen idol. Now he was twenty-one, with one of the hottest careers in Hollywood. Derek Sinclair was the son of Miles Sinclair, the movie star. Derek had made several movies now, too, and he was on his way to becoming at least as famous as his father.

"Sure," said Trevor. "Ryan's the greatest. He's into hockey. We met at a game last year. *Sport* magazine had a big party in one of the press boxes. Want to meet him?"

Of course I wanted to meet him. What girl in her right mind would turn down a chance to meet Ryan Goode? With his wavy hay-colored hair and his deep green eyes, he was definitely one of Hollywood's best looking stars.

"Okay," I said, as if I couldn't care less. "Why not?"

As we started walking over to the bar, Paige ran up to us. "The cars are here, Cassandra," she said. "It's time to go."

"Not now," I whispered to her. "I can't."

"What do you mean?" she whispered back. "Mrs. Hill expects us home. What am I sup-posed to tell her?"

"I don't know," I said. "Tell her Mr. Janelle wanted to take me and Trevor out somewhere to celebrate. Say he's supervising the whole thing and that he's going to bring me home."

"I don't know, Cassandra...." Paige began.

"Hey," said Trevor, starting to walk away. "Rio, are you coming, or not?"

I looked at Paige.

"Por favor," I begged. *"Please."*

"Oh, all right," she said with a sigh. "But be careful."

I skipped over to Trevor, and we walked to where Ryan and Derek were standing.

"Hey, Trev," said Ryan, "what's happening?"

"Ry-guy," said Trevor, shaking his hand, "how you doing, man?"

"Not bad," said Ryan. "You know Derek?"

"Yeah," said Trevor. "From one of your parties, I think."

Ryan looked at me and raised his eyebrows. "Hi, I'm Ryan Goode."

"Sorry," said Trevor. "This is Cassandra."

"That's you up there in the picture, right?" asked Derek.

"That's right," I said.

"Nice photo," said Ryan, his green eyes looking into mine.

"Yeah, that's some shot," said Derek, shaking his head. "Looks like fun."

"Oh, it was," I said. "For me, that is." I glanced at Trevor. "But Michigan here was pretty scared."

"Really?" said Ryan. "Trevor, is this true?"

"Don't listen to a word she's saying," said Trevor.

"No, really," I said, flashing a smile. "I thought he was going to lose it. Why do you think he's clutching my hands like that?"

Ryan laughed. "Watch out for her, Trev. She's going to ruin your reputation. If the guys on your hockey team find out about this, you're finished."

"Hey, keep it down," said Trevor. "What'll finish me is if the Fords find out about the hockey team."

I looked at him. "You mean they don't know?"

"No way," he said, shaking his head. "They'd never let me play."

"You're so sly, Trev," Ryan teased. "Hey, listen, Derek's having a party out in the

Hamptons next Saturday. You should come."

"Sure," said Derek. "Come on out. It'll be a blast."

"Cool," said Trevor, looking around.

"And bring Cassandra," he said, looking into my eyes again.

I smiled. I was beginning to get the feeling that Ryan liked me. I raised my eyebrows back at him. Like I said, I can never resist flirting with a handsome guy.

Just then Trevor reached out and put an arm around my shoulders, pulling me close. It was nice, but I was a little surprised, too. Then I saw a flash go off in the corner of my eye. I turned and saw the little man with the glasses, the one Trevor had been talking to earlier, holding a camera. He snapped a couple more photos and walked away. So he *was* a photographer.

Trevor took his arm away.

"Trevor, you will bring Cassandra to the party, won't you?" said Ryan. He looked at me. "You're coming, right?"

"Sure," I said. This was so cool. I was actually invited to a party at Derek Sinclair's. "Where did you say it was?"

"The Hamptons," said Derek. "You know, out at the beach."

"The beach, great," I said. "I love the beach."

But I knew there were no beaches in the city. And I also had a pretty good idea of what Mrs. Hill would have to say about my going out of town to a party on Saturday night at the house of someone I didn't even know.

CHAPTER 11

The following day, Kerri and I walked into the Cocoa Bean, a little coffee bar and cafe near the apartment.

"Come on, Cass, what's this incredible news about last night you said you had to tell me?" asked Kerri. She pulled open the glass door.

"Don't worry, I'll tell you," I said. "Let's get a table first."

But as we walked in the door, I saw that the cafe was crowded. In fact, there wasn't a free table anywhere.

"*Que mal,* what a pain," I said, looking around. "There's nowhere to sit."

"That's what we get for coming on a Sunday," said Kerri. "I guess we'll have to wait for one to open up."

"I'm going to get something to read," I said. I eyed the newspaper and magazine rack that the Cocoa Bean keeps by the counter for its customers.

"What about your news? Aren't you going to tell me what it is?" asked Kerri again.

"When we're sitting down," I said, heading toward the magazine rack. "I wouldn't want you to faint on the floor."

"Okay, okay," Kerri grumbled. "Hey, get me *Style* while you're over there, okay?"

I grabbed a copy of *Style* magazine for Kerri and the latest issue of *Buzz* for myself. As I did, I heard a familiar guy's voice behind me.

"Helping yourself to some of the Cocoa Bean's fine literature, I see," he said.

It was Jordan, Paige's boyfriend. He works at the Cocoa Bean as a waiter part-time, to make money for college.

"Oh, Jordan, thank goodness you're working today," I said. "I'm here with Kerri. Think you could find us a table?"

"Why don't you just sit with Paige?" he asked.

"Paige? Is she here?"

"Sure," he said. "She came in to meet me. When I get off work we're going to the zoo together."

I shook my head. The zoo. Imagine going to the zoo on a date. Like I said, Paige and Jordan are like little kids sometimes.

"Where's Paige?" I asked, looking around.

"Over there." Jordan pointed toward the back of the cafe.

"Oh," I said. I usually prefer to sit in the front at the Cocoa Bean, near the plate glass window. That way you get a good view of everyone walking by on the street. And they get a good view of you, too. But the back was better than nothing.

I called to Kerri, and we made our way to where Paige was sitting alone. She had on jeans, a sweatshirt, and her glasses with her hair in a ponytail. She was reading a book, with a frothy iced choco-cappuccino in front of her.

"Oh, hi, guys," she said, looking up.

"Hi," I said. I slid into an empty chair and put my copy of *Buzz* on the table. "Thank goodness you have a table. This crowd is incredible."

Jordan came over to us. "What'll it be, folks?"

"A *cafezinho* for me," I said. The Cocoa Bean is one of the only places I've found in New York that serves real Brazilian coffee.

Kerri pointed to Paige's drink. "Is that one of those mocho-choco things?"

"Iced choco-cappuccino," said Jordan, looking at Paige and smiling.

"Sounds good," said Kerri. "I'll have one of those."

I opened my copy of *Buzz* and started leafing through it.

"All right, Cass, I'm not going to wait another minute," said Kerri. "We're sitting down. Now, what's your news?"

"Okay," I said, looking up from the newspaper and leaning forward a little. "Guess who I met last night?"

"I don't know. Who?" asked Paige.

"Guess," I said. "Bet you can't!"

"Cassandra," said Kerri, "if you don't quit stalling, I'll walk right out of here and ignore you for the rest of my life."

"All right," I said, laughing. "If you're sure you don't want to guess..." I paused for effect. "I met Ryan Goode and Derek Sinclair!"

"Oh my gosh," said Kerri. Her eyes grew wide.

"Really?" said Paige.

"Yeah," I said. "Trevor's known Ryan Goode for a while. He introduced me."

"Wow, that's great," said Kerri.

Just then, Jordan came back with our drinks. Walking behind him was Naira.

"It looks like this is turning into a models' convention," he said.

"Hey, everybody," said Naira. "Mind if I join you? I just got through with a shoot that started at dawn. I really need some coffee if I'm going to make it through the rest of the day. I still have stuff to do."

"Not at all," said Paige. "Sit down."

"I'll just have a regular coffee," Naira said to Jordan with a smile.

"Sure," he said. "Coming right up."

"Thanks, Jordan," Naira said.

"No problem," he answered. "For you, beautiful, anything."

"Hey, stop flirting with her!" Paige said, jokingly.

Jordan gave her a deep bow. Paige shook

her head at him and rolled her eyes.

We all laughed as Jordan walked away.

Naira slumped down in her chair. "That coffee better come quick," she said, "or I may fall asleep right here and you'll have to carry me home."

"Gosh," said Kerri, "working on Sunday, that's tough."

"Yeah, well, the photographer wanted to shoot at a flea market, and they only have it on Sunday mornings," Naira explained. "After last night, even *I* had a hard time getting up early." She looked over at me. "*You* must be exhausted, Cassandra. That was some party."

"It sure was," said Kerri. "Cass met Ryan Goode and Derek Sinclair."

"Cool," said Naira. "They're pretty big stars."

"I know," I said, smugly. "I mean, it's not like it was the first time I've ever met a movie star. I interviewed tons of them for my TV show. But this was different, you know. It wasn't part of my work. It was more like getting to be friends with them." I smiled. "In fact, I'm pretty sure that Ryan's interested in me."

"Oh, good," said Paige, looking a little relieved. "So there's nothing going on between you and Trevor, after all. Katerina was so worried."

"Wait a minute, Cass," said Kerri. "I thought you were really into Trevor."

"Hold on, everyone," I said. "I never said I *wasn't* interested in Trevor. What do you mean Katerina was worried, Paige?"

Paige bit her lip.

"Oops, I promised her I wouldn't tell," she said. "She was so afraid you'd be upset. It was just that, when you said that thing about Ryan Goode, I figured that meant it wouldn't matter to you anyway...."

"Paige," I said, "what are you talking about? *What* wouldn't matter to me anyway?"

Paige looked down into her drink.

"Katerina told Jordan and me that Trevor was flirting with her at the party last night," she said.

"What?" I said. I shook my head. "That can't be true. No way. Katerina?"

"She felt bad about it because she thought he might be your boyfriend," Paige went on. "She didn't want you to be upset."

"Well I am upset and she *should* feel bad," I

said angrily. "What business did she have talking to him anyway?"

"Break it up, girls," said Jordan, returning with our drinks.

I glared at Paige, even though I knew it wasn't her fault that Katerina had flirted with Trevor. Jordan looked around at our faces.

"Well," he said nervously, "I think it's time for me to go do a little work. Why don't you all get back to your girl talk?"

We waited for Jordan to get out of earshot.

"Hold on a minute, Cassandra," said Naira, sipping her coffee. "Are you into this guy Trevor, or not? And if you are, what's all that stuff about Ryan Goode?"

"Well, it's not like Trevor and I are married or anything," I said. "But he *is* the Janelle boy and I *am* the Janelle girl."

"Oh yes," said Naira, "I must have forgotten. What a *wonderful* basis for a relationship that is."

I didn't like Naira's sarcastic tone. Also, I hated to admit it, but she might have a point. After all, how much did I really even know about Trevor, anyway, other than that he was cute?

Just then, something on the table caught

my eye. *Buzz* was open to the "Hip and Happening" column. It was crowded with photographs as usual. And in the middle of them all was a picture of Trevor and me at the Vault.

I let out a gasp. "*Puxa!* Look at this!"

"What is it, Cass?" asked Kerri, leaning over to see the picture.

"I made it into 'Hip and Happening'!" I exclaimed.

I picked up the paper and examined the picture more closely. There we were, in front of the bar at the Vault, with the huge clock in the background. Trevor's arm was around my shoulder, and our faces were close. He was grinning and I was looking a little surprised. It had to have been taken by that guy with the glasses.

"Let me see that," said Kerri. She took the paper from me and began to read. "It says 'Wild and Reckless Duo. Hot new Janelle jeans models Cassandra Contiago and Trevor Stone. Are these beautiful people merely co-workers, or do they "wild" away the hours together off-camera as well as on?'"

"It's so exciting!" said Paige. "I can't believe

I know someone in *Buzz*. I'll have to buy a copy for my grandmother. She'll love it!"

"Yeah," said Naira. "A mention in 'Hip and Happening.' Great, Cassandra."

I took the paper back from Kerri and gazed at the photograph. As I did, I felt a rush of feeling for Trevor. How could I have doubted that I liked him? There we were, the Janelle girl and the Janelle boy, with our picture in New York's hottest paper. What could be better?

"I bet Mr. Janelle will be happy to see that," said Kerri. "It'll probably be great for business."

"Hey, speaking of Mr. Janelle, where did he end up taking you guys last night, anyway?" asked Naira.

"What do you mean?" I asked.

"He took you and Trevor out somewhere to celebrate, right?" she said. "I heard Paige telling Mrs. Hill about it."

"Oh!" I said, laughing a little. "Paige was just covering for me."

"Cassandra wanted to stay at the party a little longer, so I told her I would say that to Mrs. Hill," Paige said quietly.

"Oh, I get it," said Naira. "Listen, I'd watch out about that stuff if I were you, Cassandra. I mean, what if you'd gotten caught and the Fords had found out? Not only that, but Paige could have gotten into big trouble lying for you. How could you ask her to do that?"

"Oh, it wasn't a lie," I said, "just a little fib. I didn't stay out that much later anyway."

"Even so," said Kerri, "what if you hadn't gotten away with it, Cass?"

"Well, I did get away with it, didn't I?" I said, taking a sip of my coffee. "And now I just have to figure out how to get away with it again on Saturday."

"Saturday?" said Kerri. "What are you talking about?"

"That's the best part of my news," I said. "I'm going to a big party out at Derek Sinclair's beach house on Saturday night."

"Gee, Cassandra, I don't know if Mrs. Hill's going to go for that," said Paige doubtfully.

"I'm sure she isn't going to like it at all," said Naira.

"Well, she can't dislike it if she doesn't know about it," I said.

"But, Cass, how are you going to get out of the apartment?" asked Kerri.

"Yeah," said Paige. "What are you going to tell her?"

I looked at them and grinned. "That's where you guys come in," I said.

CHAPTER 12

"Are you sure you know where you're going?" I asked. I peered out through the windshield into the darkness.

"Sure," said Trevor. "No problem. This is just a shortcut."

"How much of a shortcut can it be?" I asked. "We've been driving around in the woods like this forever."

"Hey, don't worry about it, Rio," he said, grinning. "You're in good hands. Don't you trust me?"

"Sure," I said, but I was beginning to wonder if I really did.

It was Saturday night. Trevor and I were on our way to Derek Sinclair's party in Trevor's little red sports car. The Hamptons were on Long Island, a couple hours outside of New

York City. It was a good thing I'd come up with a plan to get out of the apartment without telling Mrs. Hill because there would have been no way I could have made it back into the city by midnight.

Sneaking out hadn't been easy. And I couldn't have done it without Paige and Kerri. First, I had told Mrs. Hill that I had a headache and didn't feel like eating dinner. Then, while everyone else ate, I stayed in my room and got dressed in my black-and-white striped miniskirt and my black tank-top body suit.

After dinner, Paige offered to check on me and reported back to Mrs. Hill that I was asleep for the night. Then, while Mrs. Hill did the dishes, Kerri guarded the kitchen door and Paige came to let me know that the coast was clear so I could sneak out. Finally, Kerri had promised to make sure the front door was unlatched later tonight so that I could get back inside without making too much noise.

Paige had been really nervous about the plan, but I told her there was nothing to worry about. Actually, even Kerri was a little reluctant about the whole thing. But, like I explained to them, as long as they did their jobs well, Mrs. Hill would never find out.

So now, here I was in Trevor's car, possibly lost in the dark woods. However, if we did ever manage to get out, we'd arrive at a party hosted by one of Hollywood's hottest young actors. I could hardly wait. Derek Sinclair and Ryan Goode were known for hanging around with a bunch of other young stars, so if I was lucky I might get to meet some of them, too.

That is, if we ever get there, I thought. We seemed to have been driving in circles for the last hundred miles. In fact, I could have sworn we'd passed that big oak tree three times already.

Then, miraculously, we emerged from the woods and began driving along the beach. When I looked over I could see the dark blue ocean glimmering in the moonlight.

I glanced over at Trevor. He looked really good tonight in his black T-shirt, black jeans, and black leather jacket. The beach at night could be pretty romantic. Maybe tonight was the night something would happen between the Janelle girl and the Janelle boy. I wondered if there would be any photographers or reporters at the party. Probably not, I realized, since it was at a private house. I was only a little disappointed.

"That's it up there," said Trevor, pointing up ahead and to the left.

I looked and saw a huge circular white house sitting in the sand. The architecture was very modern, with tilted triangular windows and a big glass dome on the roof. Golden light and the sound of talking and laughter streamed out of the open windows. The muffled beat of dance music was coming from one side of the house. The curved driveway was filled with expensive-looking cars, and there were more cars lined up all along the road nearby.

"Pretty impressive, huh, Rio?" said Trevor.

"Sure, it's nice," I said.

The house reminded me a little of a place my family has in the mountains outside of Rio. My father flew in a special architect from Japan to design it. We used to go there on the weekends sometimes when I was little, but I don't think anyone's used it in years.

"I hope there's a good DJ," Trevor said. "Or maybe Derek and Ryan will get out their electric guitars and play for us."

"Are they in a band?" I asked.

"Sort of," answered Trevor. "Mostly they just play for friends and stuff."

"Cool," I said, thinking what a good piece of gossip that would be. I could pass it along to the girls back home. Kerri would have loved this place!

Trevor parked the car on the road and we got out. I adjusted the straps of my body suit and straightened my miniskirt, and we headed up the driveway. We passed a group of girls in long dresses walking down the driveway, giggling. Closer to the house, groups of people were standing around.

When we got to the house, Trevor didn't ring the doorbell. He just pushed open the door, and we walked into a huge circular room filled with even more people. A balcony ran around three sides of the room, and the dome I'd seen from outside turned out to be a circular skylight.

I spotted Ryan Goode standing in the middle of a group near some sliding glass doors. He was wearing a light gray jacket and a gray-and-white striped button-down shirt. He was talking and waving his arms around. The people he was talking to, mostly girls, were smiling and nodding their heads.

"Excellent," said Trevor, following my gaze around the room. "Ryan always did know about the coolest parties."

A waiter with a silver tray brushed my arm.

"Shrimp puff?" he said, offering me the tray.

"Yes, thanks," I said. I took one and popped it into my mouth.

"Let's get something to drink," said Trevor. He nodded toward the white curved bar at the other end of the room.

"Okay," I said, following him through the crowd.

On our way across the room, we bumped into Derek Sinclair.

"Hey!" he said to us. "Glad you guys could make it. The bar's over there, and the pool's through those sliding doors. You guys brought your suits, right?"

"Sure," said Trevor, patting his jacket pocket.

I looked at him. "You didn't tell me to bring a bathing suit."

"What? Oh, sorry, I guess I forgot," he said.

I was kind of annoyed. If I'd known I definitely would have brought this great new red bikini I had just bought.

"I'll take a cranberry-juice spritzer," I told Trevor when we got to the bar.

I looked around the room. There were definitely a lot of faces I recognized in this crowd. Standing by the far wall were Dylan Crowe and Michael Nash, two members of the rock group Peel. And leaning up against the piano in the corner of the room was Kara Lyons, who had starred opposite Ryan Goode in his last movie. Some grunged-out rocker types huddled together in a corner. A group of blonds with hair piled on top of their heads was dancing and singing to the music. This was great.

Another waiter came by.

"Stuffed mushroom?" he said, holding out his tray.

"Sure." I took one.

Now, where was Trevor with my drink? I looked around, but I didn't see him anywhere. Then I heard a voice behind me.

"Hey, don't I know you?"

I turned and saw an older-looking guy wearing a purple jacket standing behind me. He had sunglasses perched on his head and shaggy black hair.

"I don't think so," I told him, turning away.

"Aw, come on," he said, leaning toward me. "Didn't I meet you at Derek's last party?"

"No," I said, taking a step back. This guy's breath was strong.

"Come on, I know I met you," he said, wobbling a little. "Your name's, um, Mandy, right?"

I shook my head.

"Melissa? Susan? No, something with an *M*, right?" he said, bringing his face near mine. "Megan? Mary?"

"Not even close," I told him, starting to walk away.

"Hey!" he called after me. "Where are you going? Marguerite? Was that it? How about Missy?"

The guy's voice was fading behind me. I sighed. This could be a long night. I hoped that guy wouldn't find me again. And where was Trevor, anyway? How could he have just disappeared and left me all alone?

Another waiter came by, and I helped myself to a cracker with caviar.

A large gray-and-white sheepdog wearing a blue bandanna on its neck trotted up to me and sniffed my hand. It must belong to Derek, I thought. Or maybe one of the guests. I patted it on the head, and it wagged its tail.

Suddenly I noticed Ryan Goode walking toward the piano. He'd changed into some dark blue swim trunks and a gray T-shirt that said "Hollywood High." He was alone now, so I decided this might be a good time to talk to him. I hurried over and cut him off.

"Hi," I said, smiling.

"Hi," he said.

"Hey, thanks a lot for inviting me to this party," I said. "It's really great."

He gave me a quizzical look. "I'm sorry— oh, right. You're Trevor's friend, aren't you?"

"That's right," I told him. "Cassandra."

I was kind of disappointed that he hadn't remembered me a little better. After all, he'd seemed so friendly last weekend at the Vault. I had actually thought he was interested in me.

"Oh, yeah," Ryan said, smiling. "Cassandra. And you're a model, right? Janelle jeans.

That's how you and Trevor got together, isn't it?"

"Well, we're not really *together*," I said slowly. "I mean, we worked together on the Janelle ad, but that's about it."

"I get it," he said, smiling. "Hey, I was just on my way to the pool. You should take a dip, too."

Oh, I thought, if only I had my bikini. I could just kill Trevor right now. Here I had a chance for a romantic night swim with Ryan Goode and—suddenly I thought of something. The tank-top body suit I was wearing. Without my miniskirt it would be just like a one-piece bathing suit. Of course, it wouldn't make the same impression my red bikini would have, but at least I'd be able to swim with Ryan.

"Good idea," I said to him. "A swim sounds like a lot of fun."

"There's a bathroom down there where you can change," he said, pointing to a hall to the left of the bar.

"See you at the pool," I said, giving him a little wave.

On my way to the hall, I stopped by the

bar and ordered that cranberry-juice spritzer that Trevor was supposed to have gotten me. What had happened to him? I wondered again. It was very annoying the way he'd disappeared like that. Except it was a lot less annoying now than it had been a few moments ago. Now all I could think about was swimming with Ryan Goode.

In the bathroom, I put my drink down on the sink and peered into the mirror. Good thing I'm wearing waterproof eye makeup tonight, I thought. Now I won't end up looking like a raccoon in the pool with Ryan. I took my plum lipstick out of my bag and gave my lips a little touch-up. Slipping out of my miniskirt, I put it and the lipstick in my bag and stashed the bag in the little space between the sink and the wall. I grabbed a fluffy white towel from the stack on a shelf, wrapped it around me, and picked up my drink.

The pool was enormous. It was surrounded by a white deck with a railing. Beyond the deck, I could hear the waves of the ocean gently rushing up on the beach. Several modern-looking gray metal lounge chairs were arranged around the deck. Around the top of the railing, dozens of giant torches were anchored in place, their flames flickering in the light ocean breeze. A few people were sitting around on the lounge chairs, talking quietly in the dim light. Ryan was already in the pool, swimming laps.

I slipped out of my towel and put it on one of the chairs. As I did, I heard a familiar voice nearby.

"Hey, Marla, you going in the pool?"

I turned. It was the guy with the shaggy hair and sunglasses, the one who'd bothered me earlier.

"My name is *not* Marla," I said, gritting my teeth.

He walked toward me, a little unevenly.

"What are you drinking?" he asked, waving his hand toward my glass.

"It's a cranberry spritzer," I said impatiently. "And if you'll excuse me, I'm going swimming now."

"Hold on a second," he said. He reached into the pocket of his purple jacket. "Here, have a little something to liven it up, Mallory."

He held out a bottle of liquor toward me, his hand swaying.

"No, thanks," I said, walking away. I downed the rest of my spritzer and put the glass on the railing of the deck, near one of the torches. That guy had definitely had too much to drink. Why couldn't he just leave me alone?

Ryan was still swimming back and forth and hadn't noticed me yet. As he was turning at the far end of the pool, I glided down the steps into the water and stood in his path.

He stopped swimming a couple of feet from me and surfaced, shaking his hair out of his eyes.

"Hi," he said, running his hands through his hair. "The water's great, isn't it?"

"Sure is," I said, easing down so the water came up over my shoulders. Actually, it was a little colder than I usually like it, but no need to tell him that.

Just then, two blond girls walked out onto the deck. They were both wearing bikinis.

"Hey, Laura, April, come on in!" called Ryan. "The water's great!"

What is he doing? I thought, feeling irritated. This is going to completely ruin our romantic night swim.

One of the girls dove into the pool. She surfaced and beckoned to the other girl.

"Come on, April," she said. "Ryan's right, the water's fantastic."

April jumped off the edge, creating a huge splash. She and Laura shrieked with laughter and Ryan chuckled along with them. Then a couple who'd been sitting on one of the lounges jumped in. Soon the pool was filled with splashing bodies. This is ridiculous, I thought. I'm freezing in here, and now Ryan isn't even paying attention to me.

Just then, Dylan Crowe and Michael Nash, the two musicians from Peel, came out on the deck holding the sheepdog I had seen inside earlier. The dog was squirming in their arms.

"Throw him in!" someone yelled from the pool.

"Yeah, dunk the dog!" called someone else.

The poor dog must have known what they had in mind, because it began to whimper and squirm more vigorously. But Dylan Crowe and Michael Nash just held on tighter and kept walking toward the pool. Finally, they threw the dog, wildly yelping, into the water.

That's a pretty mean thing to do, I thought. The poor dog wasn't even a very good swimmer. I watched as it paddled, struggling, to the steps and got out. Its fur was plastered down against its body, and it was shivering. It went to lie down under a lounge chair. I knew just how it felt.

I'm getting out, too, I decided. There was no point in staying in any longer. Ryan Goode had started tossing a beach ball with a few other people. I wished I had never even gotten into the water.

But when I climbed out of the pool, I didn't see my towel. It wasn't on the lounge where I had left it.

Then I heard the voice of the guy with the shaggy hair again.

"Hey, Marcy!" he called. "Hey, you want to dance? Come on up!"

He was standing on the railing of the deck, waving my towel around, somehow balancing between two torches.

"Hey, come on," he called again. "Whatever your name is, let's dance!"

He began to kick his feet, and it was a wonder he didn't fall off. I shivered. If he has to act like a complete fool, why does he have to use *my* towel to do it with, I thought.

Suddenly, I spotted Trevor, sitting on a lounge chair in the shadows. And on the next chair, leaning toward him, was a girl with short, curly brown hair wearing white pants and a white halter top. The girl was leaning over Trevor's outstretched hand, and it took me a moment to realize what she was doing.

But then I figured it out. She was writing something on his palm with a pen!

That does it, I thought. First Trevor abandons me and now this! Not to mention the fact that my towel had been stolen by a guy who'd been drinking and that my moonlight swim with Ryan had been invaded by obnoxious, loud people and dogs. I wished I had never come to this stupid party. In fact, all I wanted to do was leave.

I turned and stormed back into the house. I planned to get dressed immediately and demand that Trevor take me back to the city.

That's when I heard it, the yelling from outside. First it was one voice, then more, all screaming the same word. But I couldn't make it out. That is, not until I saw the huge orange flames racing across the deck toward the house. Then the words were all too clear.

"Fire! Fire!"

CHAPTER 13

"All right, Miss, here you go," said the police sergeant holding out a rough-looking brown blanket. "Maybe this will warm you up a little."

I pulled the blanket over my shivering shoulders. It itched, but I was too cold to care.

"Now," the sergeant went on, "Officer Grimbell here is going to ask you a few questions."

He gestured to the red-headed policewoman at his side.

"But I told you," I said. "I really don't know anything about what happened. I was inside when the fire started. You really should ask someone else. Someone who was out there and saw everything."

"We're questioning everyone," said Officer Grimbell gently. "So I'd like you just to tell me what you remember the best you can. Please, come with me."

I followed her down the hall. All around, sitting on the hard, wooden benches, were guests from the party. Most of their faces were smeared with ashes, and a few were still in their bathing suits, like I was, shivering under itchy brown blankets. I knew that Ryan had been taken to the hospital, but I didn't see Trevor anywhere. In fact, I hadn't seen him at all since the fire had started.

Officer Grimbell led me into a small office.

"Have a seat," she said, indicating a small wooden chair opposite her desk.

I sat down, and she took a pad and a pen out of her desk drawer.

"Now, why don't we start with your name?" she said.

"Cassandra," I said. "Cassandra Contiago."

She started writing.

"And where are you from, Cassandra?"

"Rio," I said. "Rio de Janeiro, Brazil."

Then I started to get scared. I wasn't even a citizen of the United States. What if the police thought I had something to do with the fire? I could probably be kicked out of the country.

It would be the end of my modeling career forever. I began to shake a little.

"All right," said Officer Grimbell, "now why don't you start at the beginning, when you arrived at the party, what happened, and what you saw of the fire."

Suddenly, it all came tumbling out. I told her about Trevor, and about Ryan Goode, and the guy with the shaggy hair who had been dancing near the torches—I even told her about the dog.

As I spoke, all the bad feelings of the whole evening came flooding back. I'd been looking forward so much to making this big appearance with Trevor at the party and getting to know all those stars. But instead, I had ended up half-dressed and shivering, my skirt and my black bag probably burned to a crisp, all alone in a police station in a strange town. It was just too hard to take. By the time I was finished talking, tears were streaming down my face.

"Here, you go, honey," said Officer Grimbell, handing me a box of tissues. "You've been through a lot, I know. And you've given us some helpful information."

I took one of the tissues and blew my nose.

"Now," Officer Grimbell went on, "do you have a friend or a relative we can call?"

I shook my head.

"Well, Cassandra, there must be someone," she said. "Don't you know anyone who would be willing to come pick you up and take you back home?"

She picked up the phone and looked at me.

I paused and blew my nose again. There was only one person I could call, and I knew it. I took a deep breath and told her the number.

"But I think you'd better let me do the talking," I said, taking the phone.

I waited. After four rings, a voice answered on the other end.

"Hello?" I said, holding back a sob. "Mrs. Hill?"

CHAPTER 14

I could see the New York City skyline in the distance and the lights of the buildings twinkling. We'd been in the car for over an hour. Neither one of us had said anything yet. I'd been bracing myself for the huge lecture I was going to get—but now, nothing. Mrs. Hill had hardly even looked at me since she'd picked me up at the police station. Finally, I couldn't take it anymore.

I cleared my throat.

"Mrs. Hill?" I said, my voice squeaking a little.

"Yes, Cassandra."

"Um, well, aren't you going to say anything to me?"

She glanced at me.

"Well, it seems to me that you're the one

151

who should be doing the talking," she said gently.

"I just thought that, you know, I guess I figured you'd probably want to yell at me or something," I finished.

"Oh?" she said. "And why would you think that?"

"Well, probably because, um, I mean, I must have broken about a million rules tonight. I lied, I sneaked out of the house, and I went off somewhere without telling you *anything*."

"That's all very true," said Mrs. Hill.

"And on top of that, I did it all without really knowing very much about where I was going," I said. "The only person I really knew at that party was Trevor, and he didn't turn out to be a very good person to depend on. And I guess I should have recognized that earlier. I mean he wasn't very dependable before either."

"It sounds like it," agreed Mrs. Hill, raising her eyebrows. She kept her eyes fastened on the road.

Suddenly, I felt my throat tighten.

"I mean, anything could have happened to

me, right?" I said, feeling the tears from the police station well up in my eyes again. "I might have even been hurt in the fire and ended up in the hospital." I shook my head. "Going to that party was a really dumb idea."

"Yes, Cassandra, I'd have to agree with you on that, too," said Mrs. Hill.

"Then why aren't you yelling at me? Why aren't you telling me how badly I messed up and how irresponsible I've been?"

She turned to me.

"Because, Cassandra," she said, "I think you've said it all very well yourself."

I felt the tears spill down my cheeks. Why hadn't I taken some of those tissues from the police station?

Mrs. Hill handed me her handkerchief, and suddenly, I wanted to confess everything. I took a deep breath.

"There's something else I have to tell you," I said, wiping my face. "It's about that night of the party at the Vault. Mr. Janelle didn't invite us to go out celebrating with him. I just told Paige to tell you that so I could stay out past curfew."

"I know," said Mrs. Hill.

"You do?" I said, astonished. "Who told you? Was it Paige? Because if it was, I guess I don't really blame her. It wasn't very fair of me to ask her to lie like that, I know."

"No," said Mrs. Hill, "it wasn't Paige. It was your picture that gave you away."

"My picture?" I repeated.

"Yes," she said. "The picture of you in that newspaper. *Hum*, or *Ring*, or something like that, I think it was called. You know the one."

"*Buzz*," I told her, hiding a little smile.

"Yes, that's it," she said. "You left it out in the living room, and I found it when I was cleaning up. You know, there was a big clock behind you in the photograph."

"Oh, yeah," I said, remembering. She must have meant the giant clock behind the bar at the Vault, the one that said "Time to Save."

"Well, the time on the clock was twelve-fifteen," said Mrs. Hill. "So that made it pretty clear to me that you hadn't gone out with Mr. Janelle when the other girls left the party, like you said."

The clock, I thought. Of course! How stupid of me. The clock had given me away.

"But I don't get it," I said. "If you knew,

why didn't you say anything to me about it?"

Mrs. Hill turned to me. "Well, sometimes, Cassandra, no amount of talking can change a person's behavior. Sometimes, you've just got to sit back and let them learn life's hard lessons on their own."

We entered the tunnel that led from the highway, under the East River, to the city. A few hours ago, Trevor had driven me through this tunnel the other way, out to the party. But now that seemed like ages ago. I watched as the little yellow lights on the tunnel's walls flew by.

"Well, I've definitely learned *mine*," I said.

"I believe you, Cassandra," she said with a smile. "I really do think you've learned something from all this. Which is why I'm sorry to say that I will to have to tell the Fords about what happened."

A knot formed in the pit of my stomach. She *couldn't* tell the Fords about what I'd done!

"But what if they say I can't be a Ford model anymore?" I said, feeling the tears well up again. "What if they send me back to Brazil?"

Mrs. Hill shook her head.

"I sincerely hope that doesn't happen, Cassandra," she said. "But the Fords have asked me to do a job, to chaperone you girls and look out for your well-being. And I wouldn't be fulfilling my job if I didn't tell them." She looked at me. "*I'd* be breaking the rules."

I sighed. Deep down, I knew she was right. It wasn't right of me to ask Mrs. Hill to lie for me like that. Then I thought of something.

"Mrs. Hill," I said, "I understand that you have to tell the Fords what I did, but please don't say that any of the other girls had anything to do with it, okay? Paige and Kerri only did what they did because I begged them to. They really didn't want to lie at all. They were just trying to act like good friends."

"Well, frankly, I don't think they showed the best judgment, either," said Mrs. Hill. "I don't know if I'd call what they did being good friends."

"No, Mrs. Hill," I said quietly, "*I'm* the one who wasn't being a good friend."

"All right, Cassandra," said Mrs. Hill, softening. "I won't say anything about their part in this to the Fords. But I will give them a talking-to myself. And perhaps they will have to give up some of their freedom in the next few weeks to make up for it. I think it's only fair."

"Thank you," I said.

We emerged from the tunnel and onto the familiar streets of the city. I closed my eyes, suddenly exhausted. The city was still busy, even in the middle of the night. All over New York, I knew, people were out having a good time. But right now, I couldn't think of any place that sounded better than my own bed.

"All right, Cassandra, look up."

I raised my eyes, and Diane, the makeup artist, stroked some eyeliner under my lower lashes. It was Friday, almost a week after Derek Sinclair's party, and Kerri, Naira, and I were on a shoot together. We were sitting in the makeup room, wearing white cotton robes, while the photographer set up outside in the studio. Kerri's and Naira's makeup was already done, and Diane was just finishing with me.

Diane stepped back to survey my face.

"Perfect," she said.

"But, Diane, when are you doing our lipstick?" asked Kerri.

"Really," Naira joked, "these pictures are supposed to be for a Freshlips lipstick ad. Or am I at the wrong shoot?"

"Don't be silly," said Diane, tapping Naira on the nose with the end of the eyeliner brush. "Of course this is a lipstick ad. That's why Bob Martinez is going to pick out the lipstick colors for each of you. He's with the advertising firm. I'll call him right now and tell him you're ready."

She walked out of the makeup room and into the photographer's studio.

"So," I said, turning to Kerri and Naira, "guess who I finally ran into today at Ford?"

"No!" said Kerri. "You mean Trevor?"

I nodded.

"Well, and just what did he have to say for himself?" asked Naira.

"No kidding," said Kerri, making a face. "Did he apologize for abandoning you at the party like that?"

"Well, sort of," I said. "He claimed he looked for me after the fire fighters had put the fire out. He said he couldn't find me with all those people running around, so he figured I had gotten a ride back to the city with someone else. But the way *I* figure it, *he's* the one who went back with someone else, that girl I saw giving him her number."

"Wow, Cassandra," said Kerri. "I guess you must be pretty upset."

"Not really," I said. "It's funny, but I realize that there was never really anything that special between me and Trevor other than a little friendly flirting."

"Really?" said Kerri.

"Yeah," I said. "I mean, he's cute and everything, but I think I was kind of more into the Janelle girl and Janelle guy image than anything else. And so was he, come to think of it. That was why he made sure to put his arm around me for that picture in *Buzz*."

"Oh," said Naira. "I get it."

"Trevor and I will probably stay friends," I said, "and he's an okay person to hang out at parties with and stuff, but he's not really dependable."

"He doesn't sound it," said Naira. "Not if he left you stranded like that."

"Yeah," I said. "I'm just thankful that Mrs. Hill was willing to come out and get me."

"What about Ryan Goode?" asked Kerri. "Is he going to be okay?"

"Yeah, Trevor said he's out of the hospital already," I said. "He just had a few minor burns."

"And what about your meeting with the Fords?" asked Naira. "Did everything go okay?"

"Actually, it did," I said. "They were fairly understanding, considering. I'll have to be really good and follow all the rules all the time. And I have to speak directly to Mrs. Hill before I go anywhere, so I can't leave a note or get someone to give her a message. But at least they didn't kick me out or send me home."

"Yeah," said Kerri, "that would have been terrible."

"And Eileen served me this special tea," I told them. "It was mint or something. She said it was good for figuring things out."

"And?" said Naira.

"What?" I said.

"Did you figure anything out?" she asked.

I thought a moment. I had learned something from the whole experience with Trevor, Ryan, and the party. I mean, it's fun to be with someone who likes to have a good time, but it's important to have people you can count on, too.

Everyone had helped me in some way in the last few weeks. Kerri had gone shopping with me, been supportive, and never complained. Pia had helped me with my Janelle dress. Naira had tried to talk sense into me. Paige had warned me. And, now that I could appreciate it, Katerina had been worried about looking like she'd been trying to steal my boyfriend.

And Mrs. Hill had been wonderful to me in her own way. I still think some of her house rules are kind of silly, but I also know that she really cares about us. I also realized that it was pretty unfair of me to involve Kerri and Paige the way I did.

Mostly, I had realized that it was important for *me* to try to be someone that people could depend on, too.

"I guess you could say I've figured out that there are more important things in life than parties," I said.

"Wow," said Kerri. "I never thought I'd hear the 'Wild and Reckless' Janelle girl say that."

"Hey, don't get me wrong," I said, grinning. "I'm not totally through with being a party girl. But I think I'm done with being 'Wild and Reckless,' at least for a while."

Just then, Diane, the makeup artist, came back into the room. With her was a man in a black turtleneck and jeans, his black hair swept back.

"This is Bob Martinez, from the advertising firm," said Diane. "He's going to pick out your lipstick colors now."

"Hi, girls," said Bob Martinez. "Now, what I have in mind for this is to pick out a shade for each of you that not only compliments your coloring, but seems to reflect the personality that your look projects."

He looked at Naira and thought a minute.

"Okay," he said to Diane, "let's go ahead and put Sincere Cinnamon on her."

"Great," said Diane, nodding.

He moved over to Kerri.

"And for her," he said, squinting, "I think I'd like to do Perky Pink."

"Okay," said Diane.

Next he came to me. He studied me a moment, stroking his chin.

"Definitely," he said nodding. He looked at me again. "This one's definitely Reckless Red."

"Oh no!" I said, and Kerri, Naira, and I burst out laughing.

book (or **portfolio**): a collection of a model's current photos and tear sheets. Clients look at these books to choose the models they want to hire. A model's book can make or break her career.

booker (or **agent**): the person responsible for a model's day-to-day schedule. Bookers may speak to their models as often as ten times a day!

booking: a scheduled modeling job.

chart: an agency keeps one of these on each model in the computer. A model's chart lists all the options, or possible jobs, a model has coming up. It also includes any information about each job, such as rates, locations, photographers, clients, and how the pictures will be used.

client: a company, magazine, or photographer who hires a model.

editorial shoot: a modeling job for a fashion magazine.

go-see: an appointment to see a client for a specific or future modeling job.

location: where a shoot takes place.

location vans: big trailers or mobile homes that are set up at an outdoor shoot location. They're used as makeup rooms, dressing rooms, and offices by the models and the people running the shoot.

option: an unconfirmed booking.

shoot: a photo session.

stylist: a person who chooses the clothes and accessories for a shoot.

tea sheets: pages with photos from a model's editorial shoots. These are torn from magazines and put in a model's book. The better known the magazines and photographers, the more impressive the tear sheets.

test shoot: a shoot at which a starting model has photos taken for her book. A model isn't paid for a test shoot because the modeling agency hires the photographers and stylists.

"And the second runner-up..."—Eileen Ford paused—"representing the United States...is...Naira Taylor!"

For a moment, I didn't move. In fact, I don't think I even realized what was happening until the girl standing next to me on the stage reached over and hugged me. I couldn't believe it! I'd actually been named second runner-up in the Ford Supermodel of the World Contest!

First I'd been picked as one of the contest's fifteen semifinalists, then as one of the seven finalists. And it had all been leading up to this. I looked around. Standing in a row on either side of me were the other six finalists, dressed in their evening gowns. They were from all over the world, and every girl was gorgeous.

I felt kind of strange about the whole thing. I was a little disappointed that now there was no way I was going to win the contest. But at the same time I was incredibly excited. The winner and the two runners-up would go to New York City to join the prestigious Ford modeling agency.

The audience broke into applause. I smoothed down my lavender silk gown and stepped forward. Even though I'd been modeling in Chicago since I was ten, I couldn't help feeling nervous. So far this was the most important thing that had happened in my modeling career.

Not that I plan on being a model forever—I have other things in mind. In fact, my real ambition is to go to medical school someday. Modeling is just about the best way I have to save up for my education. College is really expensive, and there are four kids in my family.

Besides, my mother always used to say to me, "The apples always taste the sweetest if you water the tree yourself." In other words, it feels better to get something when you know you worked for it on your own.

Eileen Ford reached out and shook my hand. "Congratulations," she said, giving me a warm smile.

"Thank you," I said.

"Your family will be very proud," she said.

I closed my eyes for a moment and thought about my father, my little brothers, and my little sister back home in Chicago. I knew my dad really wished he could be there to see me compete, but there was just no way he could leave his business right now. He owns this big video arcade called The Fun House, and summer is his busiest time.

I also knew that everyone at home would be watching the contest on TV. I could just imagine my dad in the corduroy chair in the living room with my little sister, Kyra, on his lap and my younger brothers, Jameel and Yusef, sprawled on the floor.

The last few moments of the contest went by like a dream. Eileen announced the name of the first runner-up, who was from Venezuela, and then the name of the winner. It was the girl to my left, who was from Germany. She started crying, and I gave her a big hug. Then the contest's theme music started to swell, and the audience applauded. I had to keep reminding myself that it was real.

It was real. And soon I'd be on my way to New York City. I was one step closer to becoming a Supermodel.

THE FORD SUPERMODELS OF THE WORLD COMPETITION

With branches in New York, Florida, Paris, Tokyo and Sao Paulo in Brazil, the Ford Agency is the largest and most prestigious modelling agency in the world. Famous names on the Ford books include Naomi Campbell, Christy Turlington, Christie Brinkley, Kelly Le Brock and Jerry Hall, while in the past, the agency has launched the careers of celebrities as well-known as Kim Basinger, Sharon Stone and Jane Fonda.

Constantly on the lookout for star quality in beautiful faces, the Ford family run an annual Supermodel of the World competition, open to all 14–24 year olds worldwide, in the hope of discovering the next international modelling superstar. The competition is sponsored by fashion magazines, cosmetic companies and TV shows all over the world, and the winner is guaranteed the leap from obscurity to the pinnacle of the world's most lucrative and glamorous career.

The next Supermodel of the World? As Eileen Ford says, "You never know at which bus stop, beach or barn dance she will show up. But you can be sure we're looking for her . . ."